THREE SPANISH ANGELS

never judge a book by it's cover

GEORGE WASHINGTON COPLEY

iUniverse, Inc.
New York   Bloomington

Three Spanish Angels
never judge a book by it's cover

This is a work of fiction. All of the characters, names, incidents, organizations, and dialogue in this novel are either the products of the author's imagination or are used fictitiously.

iUniverse books may be ordered through booksellers or by contacting:

iUniverse
1663 Liberty Drive
Bloomington, IN 47403
www.iuniverse.com
1-800-Authors (1-800-288-4677)

Because of the dynamic nature of the Internet, any Web addresses or links contained in this book may have changed since publication and may no longer be valid. The views expressed in this work are solely those of the author and do not necessarily reflect the views of the publisher, and the publisher hereby disclaims any responsibility for them.

ISBN: 978-1-4502-3870-0 (sc)
ISBN: 978-1-4502-3871-7 (ebook)

Printed in the United States of America

iUniverse rev. date: 02/11/2011

CHAPTER 1

THIS IS A STORY about a lady named Eldora who had three children and their names were Nick, Lopez, and Pedro, being the mother of three little boys wasn't easy for Eldora. She had to work and make ends meet. Eldora would clean houses for people and work in restaurants as a waitress living on the out skirts of El Paso. Eldora had little ways of traveling her husband walked out on her.

When her children were very small, and because "he said there wasn't no work" and he never returned home. Nick being the oldest son asked his mother what are we going to do with papa gone. She said to him, Nick as long as we keep going to church on Sundays and keep our faith in the lord, he'll watch over us and he'll never leave us or forsaken us.

Nick replied "OK mama", then Eldora told him son listen to me since papa is gone, when anybody asks, who is your father you tell them Jesus is your father and teach your brothers what I have told you.

Nick said I will mama, I promise, and then his mama said Nick school will be starting soon. I haven't very much money. I'm going to the flea market or to a second hand store, until I get more money. I will buy you and your brother's better clothes, will that be OK son.

Nick said mama, don't worry we'll be happy like you said Jesus will help us. Two weeks pass Eldora told her three sons to sit down because; she needed to talk to them. They said what's wrong mama, she said, Nick and Lopez I bought each one of you a pair of shoes but I didn't have enough money to get Pedro a pair.

Eldora said, one of the neighbors I clean her house before said she would give me a pair of her son shoes if I would clean her house. The only problem is it will take me two days to clean her house. It is a big house.

Nick said mama, will she let you have them on credit, Eldora replied, no Nick honey, some people wants you to work first before they give you anything.

Nick replied, what is the neighbor's name that has the shoes. Eldora said that her name is Miss Scott, and then she said, she goes to our church. Nick said mama I thought it was better to give than to receive.

Eldora replied some people count their pennies more than their blessings son, so I decided to keep Pedro home until I get her house done.

Pedro said mama, please let me go to school tomorrow please, please I'll go without shoes mama. I want to be a fireman when I grow up, OK said Eldora. In two days I'll have the shoes baby.

The next morning, Eldora got her three sons up and ready for school. They ate breakfast, after they ate, each one of them gave their mother a kiss on the cheek, and said as they went out the door "we love you mama.

As they walked down, the sidewalk on the way to school. As they entered the school ground Nick and Lopez noticed the children were staring at their baby brother Pedro's feet. They heard the children taunting whispers, as two of the children which were girls walk up to Pedro and said, where are your shoes.

Pedro replied I will have them tomorrow, because my mama is working for them. Then the little girls said who is your father, Pedro replied Jesus. Then the little girls reply with a smart remark, you need to tell Jesus you need a pair of shoe's little boy, because Jesus had sandals and they walked away laughing.

That evening when school let out, they sent a note home with Pedro, saying he could not return back to school until he had shoes.

When Eldora came home after work that evening she couldn't help to notice that Nick looked depressed, what's wrong with you son, Eldora replied.

Nick said some of the kids at school made fun of Pedro for not having any shoes, and most of the children who made fun of him goes to our church. Nick said will he have his shoes tomorrow mama because he cried on the way home from school.

When I read Pedro, the note from school that he can't return to school until he has a pair of shoes. Eldora said it will be a couple of more days before; I can't finish her house, because it is really a bigger job than I thought it would be.

Nick replied, Pedro's heart will be broken if he has to wait that long mama. Why can't you just go down to Clarke's shoe store down on the other corner and charge a pair of shoes mama, you clean Mr. Clark house before just ask him.

Eldora replied Nick Mr. Clark is strictly a business man. He won't let me charge any shoes son.

Mr. Clark goes to our church too mama. Then Eldora replies you just don't listen son, drop it now! I've tried to get credit there before OK, mama said, I'm sorry said Nick.

Eldora said to Nick I'm going to the Laundromat to wash some clothes so watch your brothers OK. Nick replies OK mama. Now as soon as Eldora left, Nick told Lopez to watch Pedro, because he was going to go somewhere for a few minutes and he would be right back.

Nick quickly ran down the block to Mr. Clark shoe store and walked in and down the aisle and while no one was looking when he caught Mr. Clark back turned he quickly stuck a brand new pair of shoes under his shirt, and quickly ran out of the store and ran home as fast as he could before his mom got home.

When he got home, he told Lopez hey, look what I got for Pedro. He doesn't have to stay home now because he can go to school with us tomorrow. Lopez said this is wrong Nick. Eldora walked in and over heard the argument between Nick and Lopez.

Now Eldora saw the new pair of shoes and said oh my god, what have you done my son! Nick replied I've done a bad thing mama; I stole a pair of shoes off of Mr. Clark for Pedro to go back to school.

Eldora told Nick to get ready because me and you are going to march right back down to Mr. Clark shoe store and take those shoes back to him and you are going to tell him, what you did young man.

Eldora told Nick stealing is not god's way. Nick said to his mom I beg of you please don't do this because he might put me in jail. He does not like kid's mama; he doesn't have any kids of his own. Please mama I promise I'll never steal again.

Eldora replied I just want you to tell him what you did and you to tell him you're sorry. As Eldora walked out of the house, she took the three boys with her, and walked into Mr. Clark store. Eldora told Nick to tell Mr. Clark what he has done, and Nick had to put the shoes that he had stolen on the counter.

Mr. Clark looked at Nick and said son I except your apology, but the law is the law and you broke the law. Then Eldora said what do you mean, Mr. Clark. Then Mr. Clark said Eldora, did you read the signs in the front and in the back of the store. Shoplifters are prosecuted to the fullest extent of the law.

Mr. Clark told Eldora to many children are given a slap on the wrist everyday and they make promises by saying they won't do it again, and they get worst, Eldora so please excuse me, I have to call the police.

I'm sorry said Mr. Clark, Eldora broke down into tears, and she said please don't do this Mr. Clark, I'll pay you for the shoes and I will even clean your house as often as you want me to and for free and you'll never have to pay me a cent, and also Mr. Clark me and you go to the same church and serve the same god.

Mr. Clark replied yes we do, but doesn't one of the commandments say thou shall not steal. The police came and pulled up in front of the store, with lights flashing, while they were talking to Mr. Clark, Eldora was crying and trembling.

Nick said to his mama, I'm scared, I told you Mr. Clark was a mean man he use to curse at us when we would play on his grass in front of his house. Then the two police officer started walking towards Nick and they said little man, turn around and they put the handcuffs on Nick.

Eldora started screaming, and saying please, please he is only fifteen years old, "as the two police officer" started taking him out the door. Eldora and Nicks younger brothers started crying very hard.

Eldora asked where are you taking him, to jail lady replied one of the police officer's and you will have to go pay his bond in the morning. As the police car pulls away, Nick sitting in the back of the police car looking out the back window in tears.

Eldora said to Mr. Clark how could you do this, as he just started smiling at her, Lopez and Pedro looked at him and said why are you smiling, then Mr. Clark started laughing.

Eldora replies to Mr. Clark you are a wolf in sheep clothing, as Eldora and her two sons started walking home, Lopez said mama why did you do this to Nick. Eldora said with tears in her eyes I didn't think Mr. Clark would go this far. I was wrong.

When Eldora got back home she told Lopez and Pedro to go and do their homework. I'm going upstairs to pray, when she went to her bedroom she kneeled down beside her bed and prayed for hours, weeping and crying as she said to the lord, did I do the right thing.

Then a few seconds later, a soft voice said to her Eldora, there's a reason for all things to happen and then a comfort came over her.

After praying, she walked downstairs and asked the boys if they were done with their homework and if you are go on to bed.

The next morning, Eldora got Pedro and Lopez off to school. Then she walked all the way to the police station, and the police officer told her that the bail was set at five hundred dollars cash.

Eldora heart was broken, she asked the police officer if she could see her son before she went back home. The police officer told her yes, only for a few minutes, as she walked back to the cell block, Nick was sitting on the side of the steel bunk bed he had slept on.

Nick just looked at her, not saying anything. Eldora said, Nick are you OK son. Nick got up and walked towards the steel bars as Eldora put her hands on his hands. Nick quickly pulled his hands away, and said, you ask if I'm OK look at me mama do I look OK, I had no sleep and I watched the rats play by my bed, do you know what that it is like to sleep in a cold dark room mama.

I just wanted Pedro to have a pair of shoes mama. Was that wrong, how could god do this to me Eldora replied god didn't do this to you, I did this to you son. I'm very sorry Nick.

I'm going to the church this Sunday and ask the pastor and the congregation to help me to get you out of jail son. Nick then replied, mama those people are not going to help us, they hate us. They make fun of our clothes we wear, the children that goes there makes fun of the house we live in, even call us bad names.

Eldora said Nick, why didn't you tell me. Nick said, you told me to do unto others as you would have them to do unto you. Nick said mama, I have a bad feeling that they will punish me for this, god is angry with me isn't he.

Please tell Pedro and Lopez, I'm sorry for what I have done tell them I will always love them. Eldora said, Nick I will pray for you son, and then Nick said, no mama it's too late to pray for me, tell my brothers to never steal anything mama. Then the police officer came back there and said I'm sorry miss but it is time for you to go.

CHAPTER 2

ELDORA SAID, NICK I got to go now son. I'll try to come back and see you tomorrow baby. Nick said no mama don't come here, because I know you're needed at home, I love you Nick, bye Eldora said.

Before Eldora left the police station she asked the police officer at the front desk "what will happen if I don't get the money for Nicks bail." The police officer replies ma'am he will be held here until a court date, which will be next Monday then he will go in front of a judge for his crime.

Then Eldora walked back home crying, after she got back home she ran upstairs kneeled down beside her bed and started praying again, she said lord help me, I don't think I can take this, then surprisingly a comforting feeling came over her again, be patient my child there is a reason for all things to happen.

Then Pedro and Lopez came home from school Eldora noticed that Lopez had a black eye. Eldora said Lopez what happened, Lopez replies a boy at school said to me what kind of bird doesn't fly, then I said I don't know and the boy said a jail bird and then he laughed, then I punched him in the nose and then he punched me in the eye.

Lopez asked mama did you tell on Nick. Then Lopez started to cry, then he said, I miss him mama, and another thing he would have never done that to you. I hate you mama, I hate you, he repeated then he ran out the front door. Eldora started crying and grabbed her chess, Pedro walked over to her and said, what's wrong mama I've been having chess pain lately I'll be alright honey.

When Sunday morning came, she and Pedro got dressed and ready to go to church, then she asked Lopez are you going son.

Then he said mama what I said to you I don't really mean it I don't hate you, I just hate what you did to Nick, please don't make me go to church because, I don't feel like I fit in mama.

Eldora said to Lopez son stay home and pray for the people at church promise me son, I promise mama I will pray for them.

Eldora and Pedro started walking to church after she got there she opened the door and walked in, and sat in the back row.

The pastor was greeting people, then he walked up to Eldora and said how are you doing my most trusted angel, she replied I've been having chest pains, then she said I have been sick pastor. I need you to pray for me, I'll pray for you my child.

Then Eldora said I would like to give a testimony to the church this morning. Sure you can said the pastor, Eldora, Let me get them all seated OK. Reply the pastor, OK pastor said Eldora.

The Pastor got on the microphone and said "church" Eldora has a testimony for all of us, sister Eldora come to the front of the church please. As Eldora walked down the middle isle to the front of the church people were whispering and laughing at her. She heard one of the children make a commit, there is the shoe bandit's mother, but Eldora didn't let that bother her.

The pastor sets aside and gave, Eldora the microphone. Eldora just stirred for a few moments then she said, church, I came to you not as a sister or a Christian but as a beggar. I'm not asking for money but I will ask for my son's forgiveness.

Besides my own family, I thought I could turn to my spiritual family in the times of trouble. I'm sorry if we been a burden to all of you, see I lost my husband years ago because he couldn't take care of us, now I'm losing my son for how long I don't know. I hope and pray he can find in his heart someday to forgive me. I ask Lopez to come to church this morning with me he is ashamed of the clothes he wears.

I've always taught my sons never disrespect or make fun of anybody don't gossip, but to pray for one another. By this time the congregation was quit, listening to Eldora speak. Then Eldora said Jesus could have been born in a mansion, but he didn't want that, instead he was born in a manger. Jesus could of rode up on a Clydesdale horse, but he didn't want that, instead he rode on a jack ass. The fox had holes, birds had nests, and the son of man had nowhere to lay his head.

Church when you all tuck your sons and daughters in bed tonight, think of my son Nick, because he has to lay his head down on a cold steel bed without a pillow for the next few nights. Church please I've never asked for nothing that I didn't earn or worked for, all I'm asking for is a simple little prayer from all of you. All I want is to hold my son Nick again. At this time every-body head turned around and looked at Mr. Clark, he bowed his head down.

Eldora said, sister and brothers there been a lot of holidays me and my children walk down the sidewalk just happen to look over at people houses on Christmas morning opening their gifts, it didn't bothered us that we didn't have any gifts to open, we were happy just to have one another and a warm bed to sleep in, and a hot meal. God says love is patience and kindness.

I'm sorry pastor if I took up so much of your time with my testimony. The pastor replied Eldora that was the most beautiful message, I've heard in a long time, as Eldora walked back up the aisle; Eldora noticed the tears in people eyes and smiled at her as she sat down.

The pastor then said before I close this sermon, I want to say something "I had another message to preach but Eldora's has preached a better one and we all needed to hear the truth.

Eldora just said it all, Eldora is my most precious angel, I wish I had more like her, if the world had half the wisdom and understanding that Eldora has the world would be a better place to live in. If you didn't understand what she was saying, I'll explain it to you all. Eldora has just told us, god wasn't too good for anything or anyone it's not if we buy new clothes or, a new car, or gifts that make us, those things are not important.

They don't make us better than our next door neighbors we live beside or we sit next to. God is going to judge us by how we treat one another, helping one another and how we care for each other.

Most importantly how much we love one another.

That is what Eldora is talking about, so before I close this sermon lets pray for Eldora's health problems, and that her son will come home soon.

When service was over, the pastor and his wife stopped Eldora at the door and told her any time she needed a ride give them a call, or anything you need please just ask us.

Eldora then said I'll clean your house and the church for you all, no said the pastor, Eldora you done something today that I've never been able to do. What's that said Eldora; the pastor then said you know how to put tears in people eyes and smiles on their faces.

My child, I'm going to give you a ride home Eldora thank you pastor said Eldora. Eldora and Pedro got out of the pastors car and said thank you and we will see you next Sunday, OK good day said the pastor and his wife.

Eldora walked in the house full of joy, Lopez looking at his mama and said; how you can be so happy knowing your son is in jail. Eldora went back into a state of depression. Lopez just walked out the front door without saying goodbye.

After that night the next morning, Eldora got up to get the kids ready for school, a stranger knocked at the door Lopez answered and yelled up to his mother, mom a Mr. Conner wants to talk to you. Eldora came down stairs and said yes can I help you, yes my name is George Conner, Eldora said what is this regarding Mr. Conner. This is about a job, I want you to work for me and Eldora said I only do house cleaning.

Please let me come in and I will talk to you, come in sir, and thank you he said.

Mr. Conner please hold on and let me get my boys off to school, go ahead Eldora please just call me George, alright. Then Eldora said did I see you and some lady at church yesterday morning, yes you did said George that was my wife I was sitting with and her name is Maria.

I will double your wages for whatever you make at cleaning houses. What do you do for a living George, asked Eldora? George replies I own a pawn shop in El Paso, I will teach you how to run the business for me.

I travel a lot, give me about a month to teach you, and if you don't like it, which I know you will, excuse me George, sorry but I can't take your offer. Why said George, Eldora replies and said I can't drive and I don't have a car, no, no said George I live just six blocks over from you, I will give you a ride every day, and when I can't my wife will.

Eldora asked George will your wife like me. My wife already loves you Eldora, after you gave your testimony at Sunday service yesterday morning my wife told me to take the ad out of the newspaper, and then she said I'm going to pray that lady comes and works for us.

Well here I am said George, and if you don't come with me now my wife will come over here herself and get you. Eldora said I can't go right now, I have to get ready and go to the police station and see my son. George said how are you getting there.

Eldora replies I have to walk there, no, no, no said George I will take you there myself, and wait for you Eldora, just promise me you'll come to my house and meet my wife, OK I promise said Eldora.

George and Eldora went to the police station after they parked George said to Eldora, can I go in with you, Eldora said yes you can. As they walked into the jail, Eldora said can I see my son, only for fifteen minutes, no longer said the police officer.

Then the police officer looked at the man and asked are you family, and George replied, no sir I'm not, then you will have to stay out here in front sir, said the officer, OK said George.

As Eldora walked to the back, Nick looked at his mother very strangely and said what are you doing here old lady, Eldora said Nick, I'm your mother no said Nick, a mother would not do this to their son.

Nick please don't say things like that to me, your clothes are dirty, and do you want me to bring you a clean outfit. The pastor told me at Sunday services yesterday morning anything I need he said he would help me out.

Nick, do you want me to borrow the money and get you out of jail, do you hear me son. No, do you hear me old woman, I don't want your help or the pastors help. I don't want any kind of help from those people at that church, because they pretend to serve god and hide behind the cross all that money you gave them over the years.

Mama you could have bought me and my brother's new clothes, new shoes, even Pedro a pair of shoes, by the way old woman, where are the new clothes you promised us said Nick.

Eldora said this isn't fair son the money I gave to the church was my tidings. Then Nick said just go, please go. Eldora said, I still got a little time to talk to you son.

Nick starting screaming for the guards gets this foolish old woman out of here now. Eldora bursts out into tears as she walks back to the front then George looked at her and asked Eldora are you OK.

Eldora says to George, please take me back home, please, OK said George as they got into the car George couldn't help noticing that Eldora had her hands over the left side of her chest, all the way back to her house, and keeping her silent.

George said, are you sure that you're OK, Eldora I'll be fine once I get some rest tell Mrs. Conner I would like to meet her as soon as I start feeling better, please tell her, said Eldora.

George said don't worry, but I need to talk to you before you go in Eldora, do you need to see a doctor.

CHAPTER 3

ELDORA REPLIES, I HAVEN'T any insurance, George then said that wasn't what I asked you, because for some strange reason last night while me and my wife were praying, what I'm trying to say Eldora is that I wasn't only sent here to ask you to work for me, but also I was sent here to fill all your needs.

I am a very wealthy man Eldora, me and my wife knew about your situation and even about your son. Does your son need a lawyer or money to get him out of jail or do you need any food, clothes, or a doctor, anything.

I know you have a belief that people should make it on their own, which is good Eldora but sometimes we all need a little help. I feel that I've been sent on a mission, and I don't know what it was Eldora.

Eldora said when the time comes I promise I will let you know George, OK. Thank you said George. Then Eldora asked George I have a small favor to ask of you, anything said George.

Eldora said, would you please give me a ride to my sons hearing next Monday, it will be his sixteenth birthday, Eldora started crying again then George said, Eldora relax me and my wife will pray for you and your son.

Then she got out of the car, and said thank you George and god bless you. George left and Eldora went into the house she felt heavy with burden. Eldora went upstairs, she wasn't able to kneel down beside her bed because of the pain in her chest, and instead she laid down on the bed and her head on the pillow and started praying.

Eldora said lord I want to thank you for opening doors for the pastor and brother George offering me help, but I'm troubled lord, because Nick doesn't want the churches help, then surprisingly a voice said, I will comfort you once again my child and remember there is a reason for all things.

Then Eldora fell into a deep sleep. That late afternoon time has passed; Eldora was waken from her sons running through the door yelling mama where are you. Eldora replies upstairs, then she asked why.

Mama, you know the people at the church, their kids go to our school, we got a note from each of the childrens parents, from each kid at our school, and we had thirty notes all together.

Lopez said mama read them, and then Eldora replied since you and Pedro are so excited, I will read them for you too. When she got done reading the letters, Eldora said, boys some of the members of the church wants to take you boys shopping for clothes that you need.

Eldora replied boys don't take advantage of the church members please. The boys said we won't mama, and then Eldora said, because some of them want you boys to write a Christmas list and the boys said really mama, yes said Eldora.

Eldora noticed the boys were day dreaming with sparkles in their eyes and smiling, then Lopez said mama all I want is my very own baseball bat and glove.

Pedro said all I want is a red fire truck engine with a ladder on it. Then the boys noticed as their mother was reading the last letter and started crying, the boys said mama why are you crying.

Eldora said boys you know when we walk every Christmas morning down to Salvation Army and have dinner, then the boys replied why mama, what does that note say.

Eldora replies, my sons we get to spend Christmas morning eating at home this year, because one of the members are getting us our own turkey, ham dinner and a fruit cake. Then the boys said what would you like to get for Christmas mama.

Eldora replied I would like my first born son home for Christmas dinner that would be my gift, us to mama said the boys.

Lopez and Pedro said mama why is god being so good to us.

Then Eldora said, god sees down the road where we can't the strange thing is, there is ninety members of the church but one third of them has offered us help.

God is opening one door's after another, I just hope and pray that god will open one more door, and let me bring Nick home, praise god and the boys said amen mama.

The following day, Eldora started working for Mr. and Mrs. Conner's at the pawn shop. Eldora was very nervous then Mrs. Conner told Eldora to relax and sit down and talk to me about your family.

Eldora replied people don't get paid for talking, Mrs. Conner.

Then Mrs. Conner said Eldora please call me Maria. Then Eldora said OK Maria, were are the dust rags, mops, broom and the buckets.

Maria replied, Eldora honey we don't want you to clean, we have a maid that comes in every week that does that. All you have to do is learn how to run the cash register and put prices on the items, and open and close the store and keep me company.

Now that we got that out of the way, let's talk about your family Eldora would you mind if me and my husband go with you to your son's court hearing next Monday.

Maria asked Eldora how much is your son's bail, oh Maria, said Eldora I'm a stranger I can't allow you to do that, then Maria said, Eldora you're not a stranger you're an angel. How much is your sons bail and Eldora replied $500.00 dollars, and then Maria said no problem.

Then Eldora said Maria god has opened doors for me this past week, but one door he hasn't opened, is my son hates me because he believes that I put him in jail. I just made a poor judgment, I didn't mean to.

But when I prayed, a voice said to me, there's a reason for all things. I don't understand. Then Maria said Eldora, your son doesn't hate you, also your son will forgive you someday. We all make mistakes and sometimes we make an honest mistake. I feel that god has great plans for you Eldora, so be patient.

Eldora did my husband tell you that we like to travel sometimes.

You might have to open and close the store here. Eldora replied how do I get here and back home then? Maria said Eldora you worry too much honey, me and my husband will arrange a cab to bring you here and back home. Eldora said Maria are you and your husband humans or angels.

Maria smiled and said Eldora let me take you home now, then they hugged one another. As the week pasted the following Sunday, Eldora didn't show up for Sundays service, the pastor got concerned, and some of the people went to Eldora's house and knocked on the door.

Eldora answered the door, and said come in. The pastor asks, what happened you didn't come this morning for Sunday services. We were all worried about you. Eldora replied please forgive me every one, for not coming this morning. I decided to stay home and fast. I wanted to get the house cleaned up for my son. Nick may come home tomorrow; I baked a cake for him, and got some ice cream too. Pastor would you, and the rest of you like to come tomorrow you're all welcome said Eldora. The pastor replied we'll be here if you like Eldora, as they left each one of them said good bye.

Then the next morning, Eldora got the kids off to school, she was so happy to get ready. George and Maria knocked at the door, Eldora let them in. George said good morning Eldora are you ready to go to get your son, and then Eldora replied oh yes. They all left the house, and got into the car and on their way to the court house.

Eldora said I made a cake last night for Nick it has sixteen candles on it. Would the both of you come to Nick's birthday party?

Maria said we wouldn't miss it for the world. George replied were here, then Eldora said, as they got out of the car, I've never been so happy and nervous at the same time.

Eldora and the Conner's walked into the courthouse, they were asked to be seated until the judge called Nick down about forty five minutes later. The bailiff called out will the parents of Nickolas Santos please approach the bench. Then Eldora, George and Maria started walking towards the bench. Then they brought Nick out, Eldora smiled at him but Nick didn't smile back.

The judge looked at Nick and said son the crime you committed carries a five year sentence, how do you plea. Nick said guilty sir, and then the judge said to Nick your mother wants to take you home would you like that young man. Nick said no, I don't want to go anywhere with that old woman.

The judge replied, with that attitude son, I have no choice but to place you in a correctional center for boy's for five years. You will not be release until you're eighteen years of age, at that time. Eldora, was broken hearted again Eldora said please your honor, can I talk to him before you take him away from me.

The judge replied, Mrs. Santos I know you're a good woman. I am very sorry ma'am take all the time you want, you'll be notified in a few days about the information when you can see him, call him and if you have any problems, you let me know, Then Eldora said I will your honor and thank you sir.

Eldora asked George and Maria, I would like to be alone with my son just for a few minutes, and Then The Conners said we understand. We'll be waiting in the back for you Eldora.

As Eldora walked towards Nick, she knew she had to remain strong; she wanted to know if he needed anything, as she started talking to him.

Eldora said son can I do anything for you baby, then Nick said yes I want you to bring Lopez and Pedro to see me on school breaks, for holidays there is one more thing I want you to do for me, do you really love me, Then Eldora replied son I would do anything for you. I would even die for you son, then Nick said do it old woman, then the guard took Nick away.

Eldora fell to her knees with her left arm holding herself off the floor and the right arm holding her chest. An officer yelled out "code red" then George and Maria saw Eldora kneeling down and they ran towards her to help her up as the officer asked George do we need an ambulance.

George said no, I will take her to my doctor right now as they put Eldora into the car and took her to the hospital. Maria would turn around every now and then saying are you OK Eldora, As Eldora still was holding her chest, and when they reached the hospital.

George got out of the car and got a wheel chair for Eldora and pushed her into the hospital. The doctor quickly waited on her, the doctor told George and Maria, we need to keep her here to run some test on her, and we need to keep her over night. Then Maria told George to go to Eldora's house and get Lopez and Pedro so they can spend the night with us.

George if I have to I'll stay all night with her, will it be alright, George she has no one. George said I'll take care of the boys dear, then Maria said I'll call you if things change then George said I'll go now I love you, then Maria smiled and said I love you to.

George left, as he arrived down Eldora's street, he was having trouble getting to her house because there was so many cars on both sides of the street. He asked himself what is going on here, he finally got to Eldora house there were people on her porch and in her yard, there was no where to park and people holding up signs saying welcome home Nick.

CHAPTER 4

GEORGE SAID TO HIMSELF what should I do. I know what I'll do; I will talk to the pastor while I'm here. So George told the pastor what happen, I hope these people will understand pastor, then the pastor said to George they'll understand, because they knew she has been ill, and if Nick only knew how much he was loved, because one third of the church came. Then George said pastor can you give me some help with putting all these gifts in the house. Pastor said tell Eldora we'll all be praying for her and well help you George, as soon as they got the last gift in the house, George locked the door.

Lopez and Pedro was coming up the sidewalk, George said to himself what I am going to say to these boys. I'll figure something out OK; I know what I'll do. The boys walked up to the house and said Mr. Conner's what are you doing here? Then George said guess what your mother and my wife have some business to take care of and they'll be gone all night, so would you boys like to spend the night at my house, but first we'll get some hamburger's and milkshake's, then we can go and see a Walt Disney movie.

Have you ever seen Peter Pan, the boys said no then Pedro said I've never been to a movie before? George said I almost forgot you boys need a change of clothes don't you, then Lopez said we can wear these clothes again tomorrow because we have worn them for the last two days, we don't have very many clothes.

This bothered George and George said I have a change of plan boy's were going clothes shopping. Would you boys like that? And then go to the movies. They went into town and then they walked into a clothing store, George asked one of the clerks to size up the boys. I want the best for the boys, six pairs of jeans, six shirts, and new tennis shoes and don't forget the socks and underwear.

After they got done at that store they went to a dress shop next door and George told the clerk there to pick out two dress outfits for each of the boys and the best dress slippers money can buy.

When they got done Lopez said this is a lot of clothes Mr. Conner's, thank you so much, your welcome Lopez then they got in the car. George couldn't help over hearing the conversation between Lopez and Pedro. Lopez said to Pedro I can't wait until next Sunday I can wear a real suit to church and I won't get laugh at. I got new outfits and clothes for every day of school.

Pedro said I love these tennis shoes, my old ones mama worked for four days for that Mrs. Scott gave me had holes in the bottoms, and my socks would get wet when it rained. Then Lopez said why didn't you tell mama Pedro, then Pedro replied if I would have told mama then she wouldn't let me go to school, please don't tell her Lopez. Then Lopez said I won't tell her Pedro I promise.

George had to choke back his tears, as he listens to the boys. Then George said here we are, at the hamburger stand. Boys I'm hungry aren't you boys hungry. The boys said were starving. They ordered hamburgers, fries, and a milkshake, after they got done; George asked if they were full yet. Pedro said I'm about to bust, me to said Lopez.

George said were not done yet, let's go and see Peter Pan we'll grab us some popcorn and soda pop and enjoy the movie. After the movie was over they all left the theater, George said boys we have to go to my house, you two need to get a bath, and pick out an outfit for school tomorrow.

One day this week I would like to take you boys to my place of business, would you two like that boys. Lopez said can we go now to your place of business. Then George said it's getting late and I don't want you boys to be late for school.

Pedro said, Mr. Conner's can I ask you something, then George replied yes. Pedro what is it you want to ask me. Then Pedro said where are your wings, in the movie Peter Pan, Tinker bell had her wings and mama said you were an angel. George told Pedro sometimes we have to do good deeds, to earn our wings, and then Pedro said OK.

Lopez asked George how we are ever going to pay you back for all the clothes, shoes, food, and the movie, mama doesn't make very much money. George told Lopez, your mother doesn't have to pay me. Lopez, you and your brother has to pay me back. Then Lopez replied, how can we pay you back?

George said you boys have to make me a promise OK. George said the firsts promise is to say your prayers every night before you go to bed, second is never miss church, and the third one is finish going to school. Lopez and Pedro both replied, we promise Mr. Conner's.

They finally got to George's house, the boys said Mr. Conner's you have a very pretty house and George said thank you. After they went in, George said, boys I'll get each one of you a towel and wash cloth. Both of you take a bath, and you can sleep in the guess room. In the morning we will get up early and have some breakfast, then off to school. After that I'll check in on Maria and your mother and see how they are doing.

While the boys were taking their baths, George quickly called the hospital and Maria answered the phone and told George, Eldora is sleeping and doing well. George then said after I get the boys off to school, I'll be up there. Then he said, honey I'll let you get off the phone before the boys hear me. George told Maria I love you and good night, and then he hung up the phone.

George went upstairs to check on the boys, he noticed the boys were done with their bathes, and they cleaned up there mess and went to bed.

George went to check in on the boys as he cracked the door opened, he noticed each boy were on each side of the bed kneeling down and praying. As George listen in, he heard Pedro praying saying, god I'm so happy I got new clothes. I can't wait to show mama, and to get to wear my new suit and shoes to Sunday school.

Then Pedro continues to say and bless that Nick gets to come home soon so we can be a family again. And bless Mr. Conner, I wish I had a daddy like him. And please god gives him his wings because this was the funniest day of my life. I never knew that having so much fun, that you can get tired. So I'm going to sleep now, god I love you amen.

George quietly shut the door, and went to his room and sat on the bed. He said lord, did you hear that little boy's prayer. He said am I doing the right thing because I don't know what my mission is, but I'll be patient and I will wait on you to show me. In the mean time I'll try to do my best that I can lord and he went to bed.

The next morning George and the boys got up and ate breakfast, and then George left to take the boys to school. As he parked by the school sidewalk he said, boys have a good day as they got out of the car. Then they started walking towards the school doors, there were some children standing in front of the door.

The children looked at Lopez and Pedro and one of them said, look at the little beggars. Where did you guys get the new clothes at? Oh let me guess, Nick stole them for you two. Wait Nick, couldn't steel them because didn't they send him away.

Then Pedro replied, my brother Nick didn't get these clothes for us, an angel named Mr. Conner's did, then the children started laughing at Pedro, then Lopez said Pedro don't try to explain yourself to them, remember what mama said, pray for the wolves.

CHAPTER 5

LOPEZ AND PEDRO WENT into the school. Mean while George arrived at the hospital, as he walked in he noticed the doctor was talking to Eldora, Maria looked back at George and said lets walk out in the hallway, I need to talk to you. Then Maria told George that Eldora had suffered a light heart failure.

Maria asked George you wouldn't mind if I stay with Eldora for a few days and help her, and then George replied no, I wouldn't mind. Then the doctor walked out and talked to George and Maria. He said to them that Eldora will need someone or somebody to look after her for the next few days because from the test's I took on her, she has been under a lot of stress. So I'm going to put her on some medication.

I would like for her to stay off her feet and rest for the next two weeks, if not, the next attack could be fatal. George said to the doctor we'll try to keep her away from any kind of stress doctor. Then doctor said, have a nice day.

George said can we go in and see her now, yes you can said the doctor. Then George said thank you doctor, and then George and Maria walked in the room. Then George asked Eldora how was your stay here last night. I slept well; I want to thank-you George for taking care of my boys, Maria told me what you did for them yesterday.

I don't know how I'm going to repay you and your wife for being so good to me. I don't know how I'm going to pay this hospital bills, or how I'm going to pay for the medication I need.

As Eldora was sitting on the side of the bed crying, she also said the doctor said I have to stay off my feet for the next two weeks.

I don't know how I'm going to wash the boy's clothes for school. Then George looked at Maria she had tears in her eyes.

George slowly sat on the bed next to Eldora and put his arm around her and said; Eldora look at me, then Eldora looked at George and he said to her, do you remember the other day when I was taking you home, I asked you would you let me know what my mission was.

Eldora you said you would let me know. Eldora said, I remember then George said well the time has come and all I'm asking is for you to keep three promises. Can you do that for me?

Eldora said I'll try, then George said, the first promise is that I told your sons that you and my wife had to take care of some business last night, and you won't be lying, you really did had to see a doctor, and that is business. I didn't want the boys to worry, do you understand, and then Eldora said I understand. Then George said well we got that out the way.

Now about the hospital bills and medications this is the second promise, will you let me take care of that and to get you a washer and dryer, so you don't have to go to the laundry mat? Eldora was still crying, then George said, why do you have tears of sadness, then Eldora replied these are tears of joy.

George said, Eldora there is one more promise I want my wife to stay with you until you get better OK, and I am sending my maid to keep your house cleaned, do we have an agreement. Then Eldora looked at George and hugged him, and said yes, my angel.

Since I met you and your wife I feel that the weight of the world has been lifted off my shoulders. Then the nurse came in and said Miss Santos here is your release papers. Take your medication and follow the doctor's orders, sign your name here on the line and you can go home.

Then George helped push Eldora in a wheel chair out of the hospital, to the car as Maria helped her in the car.

George said to Maria, let me take Eldora home and you stay with her. Then I'll stop by the business and check on the place while I'm there I'll order the washer and dryer and have them deliver them to Eldora's house. Maria you tell them where to hook them up in the basement, and Maria said OK.

Maria notices that Eldora was sitting in the back seat not saying anything. Then Maria said, Eldora are you alright, and then Eldora said to Maria, I had a strange dream last night. Then Maria said, tell me about your dream Eldora. I can only remember bits and piece said Eldora, it didn't make any since in the dream.

Nick, Lopez, and Pedro are walking in the church and standing by the front doors in white cloaks and they had wings on their back, each one of them were holding swords and some of the church members started running out, I looked up again they were in front of the altar laying the swords down. Some of the members are praying over top of them.

I notice it started lighting on the outside of the church windows there were a voice saying come outside then I woke up and that's all I remember. I don't understand my dream then Maria told Eldora it could be a vision of some kind, or where you been under a lot of stress.

Eldora said, when I pray god tells me to be patient then Maria said everything will be alright Eldora, we've just keep praying and there's a reason to all things that happen. Eldora looked at Maria and said it's strange you would say that, because I get the same answers in my prayers too.

Then George said I don't mean to interrupt you ladies, but Eldora I have to talk to you while you were in the hospital, the pastor and part of the church members came over to your house yesterday to join Nick for his birthday. They brought a lot of gifts and I made sure they were all put in the house.

The pastor told me that he would pray for you they were so many cars on your street, that it was almost impossible for me to park anywhere.

I didn't want to upset you anymore than what you already were. Then Eldora said I'm not upset I'm over whelming with joy knowing my son was loved by so many. But it does upset me what Nick said to me in the court, I am ashamed to tell anyone. Maria said Eldora Nick is a child and one day he might tell you he is sorry for what he has said to you, we'll pray about it.

George said, Eldora you're home now, Maria will you please help her into the house, and I'll leave and take care of some business.I'll be back this evening then they got out of the car and Eldora said thank-you so much, my angel then George left.

As Eldora and Maria unlocked the door and entered the house, Eldora noticed all the gifts in the living room, and then Maria said Eldora where would you like me to put all these gifts at.

Eldora kept her silence and started walking toward the dining room and sat down at the table and started looking at Nick's cake. Maria walked up behind Eldora and said I don't know what to say to you Eldora, why don't me and you go and pray. Then Eldora took Maria by the hand and said please go up to my bedroom and we'll pray there.

They went upstairs to pray, then a few minutes later Maria came downstairs and started packing Nicks gifts in the basement. Then she came back up from the basement and started cleaning the rest of the house, as she was cleaning the boys came through the door from school.

Lopez and Pedro looked at Maria and asked who you are. Then Maria said my name is Maria I'm Mr. Connors wife. Then Pedro said wow our angel has a wife, then Pedro said angels can get married to. Then Lopez said where's my mama, Maria replied she is upstairs resting she was very tired.

Where is my brother Nick at said Lopez, he was suppose to come home mama baked a cake for him and were suppose to be a family again.

Then Lopez started crying, then Maria started hugging Lopez and said one day you'll see your brother again, I promise then Lopez said the kids pick on me and Pedro every day, If Nick was with us he would tell them to leave us alone. Nick always protected us.

Maria said what are the kids at school saying to you. Then Lopez said they call us beggars and make in fun of our old clothes that we use to wear. Until Mr. Connors bought us new ones, then Maria said you tell those kids at school that an angel got you and your brother those clothes. Maria said if they have a problem with it, to take it up with god. Then Pedro said that's what I told them, didn't I Lopez, yes you did Pedro.

Then someone knocked at the door, and Lopez answered the door and a man said does Miss Santos live here, Lopez said yes.

Then the man said where does she wants the washer and dryer hooked up at, Maria answer in the basement, please.

Pedro said did you hear that Lopez, were rich now, mama don't have to carry our clothes to the laundry mat anymore, because we got our own new washer and dryer now.

Then another knock came at the door, and Lopez answered the door again the second man said, I'm here to install the telephone line for a Miss Eldora Santos. Maria said please come in and installs the line next to the couch.

Pedro looked at Lopez and said wow we even got a telephone now, then Lopez said the only bad thing is Pedro you don't know how to use one. Then Pedro said, I'll learn then another knock came at the door, this time it was George bringing the maid over to help Eldora.

Maria was giving the maid instructions, George looked at the boys and said Pedro I have a surprise for you, then Pedro said Mr. Connors I don't think I can handle any more surprises.

We got a new washer and dryer and a telephone. I'm so happy, then George said OK Pedro here is your surprise, would you like to ride in the Thanksgiving parade in a real fire truck. Then Pedro started screaming I get to ride in a real fire truck, I get to ride in a real fire truck as he kept repeating himself.

Lopez told Pedro to keep it quiet because mama was sleeping. Then Pedro went outside screaming and Lopez looked at George and said, I'm sorry Mr. Connors for the way Pedro acted, Then George looked at Lopez and said, I hope you can handle your surprise better Lopez.

Lopez said what's my surprise? George said, are you ready then Lopez said yes. George told Lopez he has gotten tickets for me and you to go to a real baseball game this Sunday after church. Then Lopez started screaming, I get to go to a real baseball game, I get to go to real baseball game then Lopez repeated himself too.

George said to Maria I hope they don't wake Eldora up, and then they heard someone say I'm already awake. Then George and Maria turned around and looked at Eldora standing half way down the steps and George said I'm sorry that the boys woke you up.

Eldora said, George why do you say you're sorry, when you have just made my babies dreams come true. This is the most fun they had since you came into their lives.

Eldora started walking towards the door, to the porch the boys saw their mama, and they ran up to her screaming with excitement. Maria said boys be careful with your mother, Eldora said I'll be alright Maria there joy, brings heeling to my heart.

Eldora, Maria, and the boys went back in the house, then Pedro looked at his mama and said I'm hungry, Eldora said baby I'll go into the kitchen and warm you something up. Some left over beans that are in the refrigerator. I don't think so Eldora, why Maria.

Maria said I'll call my maid up from the basement, she is washing clothes, and her name is Miss Santana, for now on she will help you.

CHAPTER 6

ELDORA SAID, HOW IS the maid washing clothes, I don't have a washer. Maria said you do now and a new dryer, it was delivered while you were sleeping.

Eldora said, oh I didn't know. Then the maid came from the basement, and said what do you need Madam Maria. Maria said, Eldora children are hungry please warm them up some beans.

The maid replied, I'm sorry madam Maria, but there aren't enough beans to feed both boys. Then Maria said, is there anything else in the kitchen to make for the boys to eat. The maid said I'm sorry madam there isn't anything to fix for them. Maria said, let's sit down and make a grocery list then.

George said, you can go grocery shopping later, me and the boys are hungry now, right guys and the boys said yes. Let's make a phone call replied George and order some pizzas, right guys, and the boys screamed yea, yea.

Eldora replied, I'm sorry George but we don't have a phone, then George said Eldora what is that on the end of the table by your couch, then Eldora said oh my god, it is a real telephone.

George told Eldora now you can stay in contact with your son Nick. Eldora said, I can't let you do all this for me, how am I ever going to repay you for all of this. George said please Eldora don't break your third promise, you already paid us, by letting us help you, now please can we order some pizzas.

Then Eldora said, I'm sorry George, I won't bother you any more, please forgive me, and then George said that's OK Eldora. Then Maria told Eldora, tomorrow we need to call the correctional center and find out when you can see your son, and get the address so you can write him, and call him. Then Eldora heart was filled with joy again.

George asked Lopez and Pedro, tomorrow after school would you guys like to come with me to the store, the boys said yes,. Maria said to Eldora, it is getting late I would like to stay with you tonight. Eldora told Maria you are more than welcome to stay with me, but you have a husband and you should be with him. All that I ask of you is that from time to time, please check on me.

In the morning come by so we can call that place and get the information we need, then Maria said OK Eldora, here is my phone number call me anytime of the night or day, especially if you need anything. Eldora said I will I promise, and thank you so much for everything.

George said good night boys I'll see you guys tomorrow evening. Then George, Maria and the maid said well bye and good night. The following morning as Eldora got the boys off to school; Maria pulled up in her car and went in the house.

Maria said, good morning Eldora would you like a cup of java. Eldora said yes please. Then Maria said, Eldora we've got a lot to do today. First we have to call the correctional center and then goes grocery shopping. Maria and Eldora sat on the couch and started making phone calls. After Maria got done she said, to Eldora here is the address to write Nick.

Now you can only talk to him on the weekends, you can visit him the day after Thanksgiving. Maria said is that good Eldora, then Eldora replied, that is a blessing. Maria looked at Eldora and said get ready, were going grocery shopping.

Maria and Eldora came home from grocery shopping. The boys were getting out of school, the boys quickly ran home and helped to put the groceries away when George pulled up in his car and said, are you ready boys. Yes the boys said, and quickly got into the car.

George told Maria he would be back in two to three hours, and Maria said OK, then George and the boys left.

George and the boys arrived at the store, as the boys got out of the car and followed George into the store. The boys looked at George and said, wow Mr. Connors what a nice place you have. Then George said, hey, have you guys ever played a video arcade game or a pinball game?

The boys replied, no and George said let me show you how. As the boys were playing, George would wait on the customers. Then Lopez noticed while he was playing the pinball game he looked up high on the wall and saw guns hanging up on the wall. Lopez stopped playing, and walked up to George and asked Mr. Connors is those guns real on the wall. George replied, yes they are Lopez, would you like for me to get them down and show you.

Lopez asked George what kind of guns are they? George replied this one is a deer rifle, the other one is hunting rifle for any sport. Then Lopez said, will you teach me one day how to shoot a gun. George said yes, if it is OK with your mother. Then Lopez said thank you Mr. Connors.

Then George closed the store and took the boys home. After they got home, George and the boys walked in, Maria said to George, it's about time for us to go home. Eldora told George like I was telling Maria, I can't hardly wait until the weekend, and I get to talk to Nick.

I'm very happy for you Eldora, as George and Maria said good night and left. Then the boys told their mama what a good time they had at Mr. Connors store.

As the weekend came, early Saturday morning Eldora got out of bed, she heard a knock at the door. Eldora answered the door and said; good morning Maria please comes in. Maria said, are you ready for today Eldora? Yes, I can't wait till I get to talk to my son said Eldora.

Maria said let me make us a cup of java, and then you call the correctional center. Eldora asks to speak to Nick Santos and the clerk said to Eldora, I'm sorry but the staff has informed me that your son isn't done eating his breakfast yet, I'll have him call you as soon as he is done eating.

We have your number for him to return your call then Eldora said thank -you sir, and hung up the phone. Then Eldora looked at Maria and said that the clerk will have Nick call me back as soon as he is done with breakfast. So I'll wait for him to call us back. Maria said, we'll sit here and have some more java, then a few minutes later the phone rang, Eldora answered it and said hello and three to four seconds later the other party hung up without saying anything. Then Eldora got upset, and then Maria replied Eldora it could be that someone got the wrong number, be patient Eldora.

Eldora replied, you may be right Maria but before noon, Eldora got four more calls just like the first one before noon. Maria said, to Eldora let's go in the kitchen and fix us something to eat. As Maria and Eldora were in the kitchen the phone rang and Lopez answered it.

Eldora quickly went into the living room and said to Lopez; ask Nick if he wants to talk to mama, Lopez looked up at his mama sadly, shaking his head no. Then Eldora got weak and laid her head on Maria's shoulder.

Maria said, Eldora you must remain strong because you have a weak heart, you have to remain calm, Lopez and Pedro needs you, let god deal with Nick. Eldora said it just hurts me Maria.

Lopez was talking to Nick, as Eldora and Maria sat on the couch waiting till Lopez got off the phone, because Eldora wanted to know what Nick had to say. When Lopez hung up the phone, Lopez looked at his mama and said I'm sorry mama, because Nick didn't want to talk with you, are you mad at me mama. Eldora replied, no baby just tell me what all Nick had to say.

Then Lopez said, I told him that we were coming to see him after Thanksgiving. Nick said he wanted to see me and Pedro; he wants to talk to us mama. Then he asked how we were doing in school.

Lopez told Nick about mama's new job and about Mr. and Mrs. Conners and that's about all we had to talk about mama. Eldora said did he say anything about me baby, then Lopez said no mama. Nick said he doesn't want anything from you, then

Eldora started crying then Maria put her arms around her.

Maria said Eldora remember what god said to you, there is a reason to all things. Tomorrow I want you to come to work with me said Maria. I'll pick up some stamps, envelopes and paper, and when you're not busy you can relax and write your son OK Eldora.

Eldora said I just can't understand why Nick is doing this to me. Maria said, Eldora you must remember god is in control OK. Eldora said Maria what would I do without you, you are such a comfort. Maria said, just be ready in the morning and I will pick you up.

The following morning Eldora got up and got the boys off to school. Maria came by and said are you ready, yes said Eldora.

Eldora learned very quickly, how to wait on customers, how to operate the cash register and pricing the items in the store.

In Eldora spare time she would sit down and write Nick every chance she got. As time went by the weekend came, George stopped bye and got Lopez and went to his first professional baseball game. After the game was over, George brought Lopez back home.

Lopez walked in the house and said, mama look at my new baseball jacket. It has the name of the team Lobos on it. Then Pedro said I can't wait till I get to ride in the parade on the fire truck, then George said be ready Pedro that day is coming soon.

The following morning the boys got up for school, Eldora told Lopez to put her letter out on the mailbox, and then the boys went to school. As the boys got to the school doors, one of the children looked at Lopez and said that is a nice jacket Lopez where did you steal it from.

Pedro tried to explain to the kids where the jacket came from, Lopez looked at Pedro and said, just drop it Pedro their always going to pick on us. Besides that, I hate this school; I can't wait till Nick gets out, and so we can get even with these guys.

Pedro replied we were supposed to pray for them, and then Lopez said I'm tired of praying. I want to get even and one day I will get even.

Pedro looked at Lopez I'll get to ride a real fire truck this weekend. I get to go and see Nick; I have so much to tell him, how much I miss him and how much I love him. I just wish he could see me when I get to ride the fire truck. Then Pedro started crying, don't let anyone of these guys see you crying said Lopez.

Pedro said if Nick was here he wouldn't let these guys call me names like bum, thief and beggar. Please tell me is it my fault that Nick is in that place. No said Lopez, because Nick would have done the same thing for me. Now cheer up Pedro, the bell is ringing.

We'll get to see Nick soon go to your classes. Later on that evening, the boys came home from school. The maid, made Lopez and Pedro something to eat, later Eldora came home she noticed that Pedro ate his food. Then Eldora asked Lopez why he didn't eat his food, Lopez said I wasn't hungry.

Lopez told his mama, something is bothering me this morning. Mama I know you're ill and I love you more than anything please don't be mad at me, Pedro started crying because he feels like it's his fault that Nick is gone. But it's not Pedro's fault it's your fault, please don't hate me mama.

I just don't understand why god is doing this to us, what did we ever do. I'm so confused mama. Then Eldora said, Lopez please don't let me lose you to son, I don't have an answer for everything.

CHAPTER 7

LOPEZ, IF I COULD have done it over again, I've never would have taken Nick down to Mr. Clark shoe store that morning. I wish I just went down there myself, and paid him myself. See son we all make mistakes, and we all learn from them. God didn't do this to our family I did, I know god has forgiven me, I pray that Nick will someday forgive me too.

No Lopez I could never hate you or your brothers, I can only hate myself for what I have done, and son I'm glad we had this conversation. Do you still love me son, then Lopez said mama I will always love you.

Mama I just feel like me and Pedro doesn't fit in at that school and I hate that school because they make fun of us the entire time mama.

Eldora said, look at me and listen to what I'm about to tell you when Jesus was in this world people made fun of him and laughed at him. Do you reckon if he ever felt that he didn't fit in Lopez, yet he didn't hate no one. When he hung on the cross, he looked down on them with love even though some of them hated him. I have told you son, pray for them OK Lopez.

Lopez then said mama I need to pray more, because I'm starting to think and act likes my enemy's. I just realized that this is not god's way mama. I want to go upstairs and pray, and mama I'm glad we had this conversation to. Lopez told his mama he was hungry and went into the kitchen to eat.

George pulled up in the car and got out, he had something hid behind his back, as he walked up on the porch and said where is Pedro. Eldora yelled for Pedro to come out of the house, then Pedro came out, and George looked at Pedro and said hey little guy are you ready for the big day tomorrow.

Then George said what does every fireman got to wear when they are in a fire truck, Pedro replies a hat.

George then pulled out from behind his back a bright red fireman hat, and Pedro jumped for joy. Then George said little man be ready in the morning because we all are going to the parade to watch you ride that fire truck.

After the parade were all going back to my house to have a big Thanksgiving dinner, Then Eldora said George I have a turkey and ham and other food here. George said, Eldora do you remember the third promise, yes I do said Eldora.

Then George said to Pedro, will you please go inside the house I need to speak with your mother. Pedro said OK. George sat down next to Eldora and asked her has Nick ever called or wrote her back. When Nick calls he only talks to his brothers.

I been writing him every day, he hasn't wrote me once, it's been almost three months now since I've seen my baby, and I'll never stop writing him. I know in my heart, that god will give him back to me. George said, Eldora when you go and see him please remember you still have Lopez and Pedro to take care of.

Don't worry George said Eldora because the boys already told me that Nick only wanted to talk to them? I just want to let him know that I came because I still love him, I always will until the day I die. George said, Eldora I can overrule the judge decision. I know a good lawyer that will bring your son home, no said Eldora, Nick doesn't want to come home.

When Lopez was on the phone the other day talking to him, Lopez told me after he got off the phone with Nick. Lopez looked at me and said, mama Nick said when he gets out he is going to get a job and come and take me and Pedro with him, because he said that you were a crazy old woman.

So George do you see what I'm going through. But thank you George you've been so kind then George said Eldora, I don't understand a lot of things, but one thing I know for sure, you're not a crazy old lady.

Listen I got to go now, so be ready in the morning because we will have a long day tomorrow, OK Eldora. Then Eldora said good bye George see you in the morning. The following morning, George and Maria came over. George came in and said are we ready to go Maria is waiting in the car for us.

George said Pedro; I see you got your hat on young man so out the door they all went. When they arrived at the fire department, a fireman walked up and said to George, where is the new member of the team at. Then George said he's right here Tom. Then Tom said to Pedro get your hat on son and get on the fire engine with us. Pedro ran to the fire truck and one of the firemen picked him up and sat him on his lap, on top of the fire truck.

As the fire engine pulled out, George drove behind the fire truck as they were driving up the street, Eldora was watching Pedro on top of fire truck and said to Maria thank you for making my little boys dream come true, look at him just smiling and waving at the crowd.

As they drove a little further, they were some kids standing on the sidewalk from the same school that Lopez and Pedro went to, the children were watching the fire truck go by and they recognized that Pedro was on top of the fire truck and they started shouting, look there's the little beggar, they kept repeating it.

Then George heard what the kids were saying to Pedro, and then quickly Pedro looked at Tom the fireman and said, with tears in his eyes sir I'm sorry if I messed up the parade ride, but please stop the fire truck and let me down and go to my mama.

Tom said, listen you're a fireman you're not a beggar, but I will stop the truck. Then George was very angry and he stopped the car, and got out and walked up to the children he looked at them and said, I know most of your parents and when I see them in church this Sunday. I'm going to tell them that you all have just turned a little eight year old boy dream into a nightmare.

Also gave him a memory that will haunt him the rest of his life. Then Tom looked down at George and said, I have a better Ideal George, let's give those guys a memory that will haunt them the rest of their lives. Then George said what you suggest we should do.

Tom said; let me ask the commander chief what we should do, who is that George said. Then Tom said Mr. Pedro Santos, and then Tom said attention all firefighters please stand in line and salute the commander.

Then all twelve fireman stood side by side like soldiers with their long handle axes on their right side of their shoulders facing Pedro on top of the fire truck, mean while in George's car , Lopez said to his mama I told you mama the kids were mean to us.

Eldora said to Lopez god is in control, and then Maria said you're not kidding as Maria looked in her rear view mirror. Here comes the police, the El Paso news team, and a whole lot of people. Let's get out of the car and see this for ourselves. Maria, Eldora and Lopez got on the side of the fire truck with George.

Tom was acting like a general talking to Pedro, shouting commander Pedro sir, who is on top looking down on the ground at the criminals, and look who is crying now, not you sir, and they better not even think about running away, because I have twelve of the meanest fire fighters in the state of El Paso Texas, sir.

Sir, a few minutes ago, they were calling you a beggar, but who is begging the police not to take them to jail, not you sir. You have the power sir to prosecute these criminals for obstruction to the parade sir what is your answer, and what you would have us to do. Then Pedro whispered to Tom, what does prosecute mean, then Tom told Pedro it means you can have them put in jail, and they'll never bother you or your brother again. Then Pedro said, can I just talk to them sir. Then Tom said go ahead Pedro, then Pedro looked at the school children and said Mr. Tom the fireman told me I have the power to send you guys to jail.

I'm not good at explaining things, but what I can see. I look at you guys are scared and crying like Nick was that morning before they took him to jail. I wish I had the power that day to stop it from happening. I know you guys hate me and my family.

I could never hate you guys, mama always told me and my brothers, to do on to others as you would have them do unto you. As Pedro was talking you could have heard a pin drop. As George looked around, he noticed some of the crowd was wiping their eyes, even some of the firemen.

Pedro said I didn't know my father, he left us when I was a baby, and I didn't know what fun was until I met Mr. Connors, he is the closest person to a father I ever had. When the camera turned to George he was wiping his eyes too.

Pedro looked at Tom and said Mr. Tom sir; I don't want to put their families through what me and my brother and mama have been through. We are supposed to love our enemies, I don't want this power, and will you let them go sir, please.

Tom replied, yes sir consider it done sir. Then Tom looked at the children and said, before I let you all go, I want you guys to get a good look at me and my men, keep this memory and never forget the look in their eyes. The children looked at Tom and the children notice Tom and the firefighters had anger in their eyes.

Tom said if I ever hear that any of you kids disrespect my little commander, you have disrespected all of us, me and my men will find you and put the fear of god in you, now get out of my sight.

Tom said it would be an honor if Miss Santos and her other son would join us for the ride in the parade, head east men, and help the lady up here.

They were helping Eldora get on top of the fire truck; a lady reporter looked up at Tom and said can we get a comment from you sir. Sorry lady we don't have the time, me and the commander has a job to do, Tom said.

Then the lady left, after everybody got seated on top of the fire truck, Pedro noticed that they weren't moving yet. Pedro looked at Tom and said why we are not moving yet. Tom replied, sir you didn't give the order to move out sir.

Then Pedro said OK, he screamed out, move on out. All of the firemen looked at Pedro and smiled, and then Pedro whispered to Lopez and his mama and said, I am a commander now.

After the parade was over, the fire truck went back to the station. George pulled in and parked, as they were helping Eldora down from the truck. Lopez and Pedro started walking towards the car, and then Tom yelled out, commander you're not done yet.

We want you and your brother to take a picture with me and the firemen before you leave sir. After they took the picture, Pedro shook each of the fireman's hand and said good- bye. Then Tom walked up to Pedro and said I would like for you and your brother to ride in the Christmas, and New Year parade with us.

Would you like that, they both said yes sir. Then Pedro said to Tom, thank- you for making my dream come true and then he hugged Tom, then he said good- bye. Pedro and Lopez got into the car.

George told Maria, I'll be back in a short; I'm going to talk to Tom for a couple of minutes. Then we will go to the house for dinner, as George walked into the station and into Toms office, he said to Tom I'm sorry I didn't get a chance to thank- you for what you did for Pedro, you're welcome George said Tom.

George when those bullies was calling that little boy names, I had to step out of line, when I saw those tears coming out of that little mans eyes. I wish you could feel the anger that me and my men felt. We wanted so bad to jump down off the side of the truck and whip those idiots.

George said Tom when me and you were kids you were always a show off, but how ever, you did save the day from a disaster.

CHAPTER 8

GEORGE I MEANT WHAT I said, I want that little man to let me know if those bullies ever pick on him again. Don't worry Tom I'll keep you informed, said George. Then Tom said, hey George who is living a nightmare now, it isn't that little man, and another thing George I don't have the heart that little man has.

I would have put them in jail. I know Tom; it's a good thing that you made him a commander chief, said George. Then Tom said George when you told me what happen to that little mans older brother, I've told my family, neighbors, and my employee's not to ever buy shoes from Mr. Clark shoe store again.

Oh by the way George watch the news tonight, and pick up a news paper tomorrow, because that little speech he made, I've been informed has made it big, so tell gods little angel, I proud of him. I will say George.

George said oh, I almost forgot I got to get going, I have a big Thanksgiving dinner waiting at home, oh once again Tom thanks again for what you did today and have a happy Thanksgiving Tom, you to George said Tom.

Then George rushed out to the car, and said I'm sorry I took so long guys, then Maria said to George get us to the house, were starving. On the way to George's house, he told Pedro, Tom told me to tell you he was proud of you. We will watch you on the news tonight, and to pick up a newspaper tomorrow.

That speech you made has drawn a lot of attention. Said George, Wow, I'm going to be famous mama, I use to be a nobody and now I'm a somebody, not in my eyes son, you've always been mama's little angel, said Eldora.

Then Pedro said I can't wait till I get to see Nick tomorrow mama, and tell him all the great things that have been happening in our lives lately. We are going to see Nick tomorrow, aren't we mama.

Then Eldora said to Pedro, son Nick doesn't want to see me, he only wants to see you and Lopez. Then why are you going mama. If Nick doesn't want to see you said Pedro. Then Eldora said, so I just want to let him know that I'm there for him, when you talk to Nick tell him, I still love him.

Lopez and Pedro said we will mama, and then George pulled into the drive way of their house, everyone got out of the car. As the door opened to the house the maid, Miss Santana looked at George and Maria and said the telephone has been ringing like crazy.

The El Paso press wants you to call them; Pedro is all over the news sir. Well George said, listen Miss Santana, take my calls tell them that I will call them later, because me my wife, Eldora, Lopez and our little commander are going to sit down and enjoy this great Thanksgiving dinner you have prepared for us.

I want you to sit down and enjoy the dinner with us Miss Santana, because today is a very special day for all of us. Please Maria, say grace and let's eat. After everyone is done eating, George said Eldora and Maria take the boys in the living room, and turn on the television, while I call some of these people back.

When George got done talking on the phone, he went into the living room he noticed everyone was being quiet watching the news on the television, except Pedro.

Pedro looked at George and said, Mr. Connors looked at me, mama, Lopez and you, and we are on the news, isn't that great. Then George replied, I've got more good news Pedro the El Paso press wants to come over your house tomorrow and talk to you, but I told them they would have to wait till Monday after school.

See tomorrow were going to see Nick right Eldora, then Eldora said with a smile, oh yes George. George I want to thank you and Maria for a great time today. I also want to thank you both and Miss Santana for a great Thanksgiving dinner, but if you don't mind would you please take me and the boy's home in case Nick calls.

Then George said anything you say Eldora, are you ready to go now. Yes said Eldora, on the way out the door, Eldora asked Maria, will I see you tomorrow morning. Oh yes said Maria, then George took them home.

The following morning, George and Maria came and picked up Eldora and the boys as they were traveling, Eldora remained quiet while George was driving. Maria said Eldora, why are you so quiet, aren't you excited about going to see your son. I am said Eldora.

I know in my heart, he doesn't want me there; I want Lopez and Pedro to be able to see him and talk with him. Lopez said don't worry mama me and Pedro still love you. I know my son, said Eldora.

Pedro said, mama I wonder what Nick looks like, it's been a long time since we seen him. But I want him to see my picture with Mr. Tom and the fire fighters. I can't wait till I get to show it to him; I can't wait to show him my Lobos jacket said Lopez.

George said, here we are Lopez and Pedro everybody got out and walked in but, Eldora. Maria said Eldora what's wrong, I'm feeling weak and nervous, relax and hold my hand. I will walk in with you, said Maria.

The guards told George and the family to have a seat. He asked George, who you are all here to see, Nick Santos my son said Eldora. Then the guard looked at Pedro and said, are you the little boy that was on television yesterday, it's hard to believe you're his brother.

George said, what do you mean by that, I'm sorry sir for saying that, but all of you please follow me down this hallway, and on the left side is the visiting room, please sit in the very back and I will go get Nick. It will only take five minutes, please be patient, as everyone was sitting, Eldora said Maria I'm very nervous, don't worry said Maria.

Eldora said I've never been so nervous and confused at the same time. I don't know whether to stay or run, I feel so loss Maria. Then Lopez said mama don't feel that way, because me and Pedro needs you if Nick still loves you or if he doesn't the most important thing is we need you mama.

Then George said, Eldora get a hold of yourself now, because like you said, god is in control. Then Eldora said, my sons please tell Nick to come back to me, because I need him.

Then Maria said Eldora, do you want me to take you to the car, I'll sit with you, then the door opened slowly everybody got quiet when Nick walked into the room with the guard. Nick looked at everybody for a few seconds, then Maria whispered to Eldora, oh my god he looks like a handsome prince Eldora replied I know he's handsome he looks just like his father .

Then Eldora remained silent just smiling and stirring at Nick. Lopez and Pedro looked at each other, and said wow look how tall he is. Then Nick whispered something to the guard. Then the guard walked over to the family and said Nick only wants to talk to his brothers, if you don't mind waiting in the lobby please.

George said can I talk to him for a couple of minutes you can try said the guard, as Lopez, Pedro and George walked over to Nick. George said hello my name is George Connors, then Nick said I don't care who you are, are you family. I don't think so, leave with your wife and take that old woman with you.

Maria looked at Nick and said you don't deserve a mother like her; you're a monster young man. Then Nick shouted to the guard, get them out of here. I just want to be alone with my brothers. As the guard took George, Maria, and Eldora out of the visiting room, he shut the door behind them, on the way back down the hallway.

George looked at the guard and said, I've never been so embarrass in my life of anything , what that young man said to me, then the guard said, as I told you earlier sir, it's hard to believe those boys are brothers.

Eldora looked at Maria and said can we just go to the car and wait, because I feel so weak. They all went to the car, while Nick was talking to his brothers. Mean while, in the visiting room, Nick said hey I sure do miss you guys. We miss you to Nick said Lopez and Pedro.

So Pedro how does it feel to be in the spot light, said Nick. What do you mean Nick said Pedro, I saw you on the television yesterday. Pedro how could you just let them guys go, don't you realize those kids are the ones that made fun of us growing up.

They are the ones who made fun of the patches that mama sewed on our clothes. They made fun of the house we live in; you had the enemy in your hands and just let them go. Stop it Nick said Lopez, he already blames himself for you being here, and that's enough and another thing. I don't like the way you talked to Mr. Conner's he is like a father to us.

Don't you even compare him to our father, because you didn't know our father? Papa didn't walk out on us; mama kicked him out because he couldn't get a job. People felt that he wasn't good enough to work for them in that town.

You were very young, and Pedro was just a baby. This Mr. Connors doesn't love you, he feels sorry for you. That's why he helps you; Then Pedro said that's not true. He does love us; he took me and Lopez to his store-bought us new clothes, to the movies. He took Lopez to a real baseball game, and his firemen friends made me commander in the parade.

Mr. and Mrs. Connors bought mama a new washer and dryer, even got her a telephone, and even gave mama a job. They have a maid named Miss Santana that helps her sometimes. Then Nick got depressed and said, I guess this Mr. Connors is a great guy.

You want to know something, in this place they teach me how to make dress clothes, I make twenty five cents an hour.

I already have sixty nine dollars saved, and I figure by the time I turn eighteen years old, I'll have enough money to start my own clothing store, and to get my own place.

Lopez asked Nick, why are you so angry with god. I'm not angry with god, said Nick. I'm angry with the people that pretend their serving god only on Sundays.

They give god one day, when they should be giving him seven days a week. What do you means Nick, said Lopez. Then Nick said Sunday they pretend their living for god, and then from Monday through Saturday they hide behind the cross and the altar.

They get drunk, high on drugs, or cursing one another, cheating on one another. The people at church they judge you not by the spirit you have, they judge you by the clothes you wear if you don't have decent clothes or decent pair of shoes they make you feel that you're not good enough to go there. Did you tell Mama Nick, said Lopez. No I didn't said Nick; I didn't have to, because she knew already. That's why I'm so angry with her; I made one mistake, because I wanted my brother to have a pair of shoes to go to school in.

Listen to me Lopez and Pedro, I will always love you guys. Never forget me remember who was the one that carried the black eyes and busted noses many of times for you guys.

It sounds like you guys don't need me anymore. Then Lopez said, Nick we need you, we will always need you. Mama needs you to Nick, she is sick. I'm sorry Lopez, but I can't find it in my heart to forgive her said Nick.

Then Lopez said it wasn't mama's fault, then Nick got angry and said, it was her fault you know that.

CHAPTER 9

I WAS HAVING A good time sitting here talking to the only family I have left. You have to bring that old woman up here, Lopez replied that old woman is your mama, Nick quit calling her that. Mr. Conner can get you a lawyer and bring you home, Nick why are you being so stubborn.

Then Pedro started crying, and said guys don't start arguing. Then Nick replied I don't want that old woman's help. I don't want this Mr. Conner's help either. It was bad enough that mama betrayed me, and you and Pedro are the only family I have left.

I feel that you guys have betrayed me also, and then Nick started crying. I know I'm going to regret this, for what I'm about to say, I've always been there for you guys. You guys can't be here for me. I'm dead to both of you, please leave, I want you both to leave and never come and see me again.

Then as Lopez and Pedro got up to go out the door, they looked back behind them and watched as Nick laid his head down on the table crying. As they shut the door, they walked down the hallway holding back their tears. They got outside; walking towards George's car, George, Maria, and Eldora could tell the boys were upset by looking at their eyes.

As the boys got into the back seat with their mama, Eldora said what is are wrong Lopez and Pedro. Then Lopez said, please mama not now. We'll talk when we get home. Then Maria looked over at George and shook her head for George not to say anything. No one spoke on the way home, as George pulled up at Eldora's house.

Eldora and the boys got out of the car to go in; Eldora looked up at George and Maria and said I'll give you all a call later. I'm going to find out what happened. Then George told Eldora if you don't mind, can I come over later and talk to the boys.

Eldora replied I don't mind George. As George pulled away Eldora went into the house and sat next to the boys. The boys were on the couch as she sat down beside them and asked what happened. Why are you and Pedro so upset?

Lopez looked at his mama and hugged her and said, mama I can't hate you. Get a hold of yourself Lopez, and start from the beginning. And tell me everything that Nick said. Then Lopez told her everything that Nick said.

After he got done, then Eldora looked at him and said, son it is true about your papa leaving. But Nick didn't know everything about his papa. I didn't tell him everything, I was ashamed to. I didn't want you boys to know the truth about your papa, he wanted to move from town to town, and I prayed that god would help me to get a home for you boys. God answered my prayers, he help me to get this house.

When papa did find work, he would go out and spend it on other women. I found a good church to go to, and your papa wanted me to sell this house. I told him no, because I wanted a life for you boys. I didn't want you boys to follow in his footsteps. I didn't want you boys to grow up and be like your father Lopez.

I would go out to find houses to clean or work as a waitress. What little money I did make, I would put meals on the table for you boys. Eldora looked at Lopez and Pedro and said, papa wanted to live his wild life, and I couldn't put up with it any longer.

Papa looked at me the last time I saw him he said to me are you going to sell this house, I said no then he replied it's either me or this house. Then I said to him I'm not moving and that was the last time I saw him. I did what I felt I had to do Lopez and Pedro, do you understand me.

All the things that Nick said to you boys don't bother me anymore, he has hurt me so much, that it doesn't hurt anymore. I feel that god has put comfort in my heart to not let it bother me anymore. Then Lopez said to his mama, I understand why you had to let papa go.

Then Pedro said mama guess what, I'm hungry mama can we eat, OK Pedro replied Eldora. I'll go into the kitchen and make us something to eat. As Eldora got done cooking, she put the food on the table. After they prayed, they began to eat. When they were almost finished eating, they heard a knock on the door.

Pedro opened the door and said its Mr. Conner's mama. Then Eldora replied tell him to come in. George went in and sat on the couch, Eldora said to George would you like to eat with us. George replied no thank you Eldora, I had already eaten. But if you don't mind I would like to talk to my boys. Then Eldora replied, I don't mind if you talk to them George.

Then when the boys were done eating, they got up from the table and went to sit on the couch beside George. George pulled out the newspaper, it had Pedro's picture on the front page. It read "A true little angel on wheels." Then George said what do you boys think of that.

The boys sat quietly not saying a word, and then George replied, what is wrong. Then Lopez said, is it true that you don't love us. Nick told us that you don't love us, that the only reason is you feel sorry for us. George replied to Lopez and Pedro, how can your brother say that about me, when he doesn't even know me.

Listen to me guys, from the moment I meet you and Pedro you two boys are everything I want in a son. But then again, why would I want a son when I have you two boys in my life. There is not a thing that I wouldn't do for you boys. Then Lopez said to Mr. Conner's, I will always care about you and Mrs. Conner's but please don't help us anymore.

I feel that I have betrayed my brother Nick. Then George said I understand Lopez. I know I can never take the place of your brother or your papa. But I will always be here for you boys if you ever change your mind. George looked at Pedro and said do you feel the same way Pedro. Then Pedro didn't answer. Then George said I guess you do, Well I guess I better be going now.

George looked at Eldora and said are you still going to work for us, Eldora knotted her head yes. Then George left without saying a goodbye. Then Pedro said do we have to treat Mr. Conner's like that, and then Pedro ran upstairs. Lopez replied I'm going upstairs and try to cheer up Pedro.

Eldora replied; let him be if Nick had his way he would have you and your brother hating the world. Then Lopez went out on the porch and sat down on the steps the rest of the evening. Thinking about what he said to Mr. Conner's.

The next morning, Eldora got up and got ready to go to work, then she got the boys up and off to school. On the way to school, Lopez looked at Pedro and said I'm sorry for what I said about Mr. Conner's yesterday. Then Pedro replied that's OK Lopez. On their way up the sidewalk, the children looked at them, and started laughing. They heard one of them say, woo, we better watch out for the fire commander.

Then Lopez and Pedro walked into the school, then Lopez looked at Pedro and said, not one of these guys appreciate what you did for them Pedro.

Nick was right you should have put them all in jail little brother. These guys aren't going to change Pedro. But I am. It still bothers me what Nick said to us. That he was dead to us, it also bothered me when I walked out and seen him crying on the table yesterday. Pedro, would you like to be with our brother Nick. Pedro replied what you mean. How can we be with our brother?

Then Lopez replied we are going to skip school today. I'm going to get even with Mr. Clark. The two brothers walked out of the school and back down the sidewalk. They went up seven blocks up the street, as they stood across the street looking at Mr. Clark shoe store.

Lopez looked at Pedro and said, look at that dump truck let's get some rocks off the back of it. Lopez looked at Pedro and said this rock is for Nick. Then Lopez threw it and hit the right side of the door. The glass shattered inside and outside of the store. Then he kept throwing rocks until all of the windows were broken out.

People were coming out of their place of business, looking at the broken glass. Then Mr. Clark pulled up in front of his store. He asked the people what happened to my store, then the people pointed across the street, he saw Lopez and Pedro.

Mr. Clark said, I know you little brats, you boys are Eldora kids. I like to know how your mother is going to pay for my broken windows. She can't even afford to buy you little brats a pair of shoes. Then Lopez got very angry, and picked up another rock. Lopez replied, the same way she can't afford to pay for a broken windshield. Lopez threw the rock as Mr. Clark watched the rock come down and hit the windshield as it shattered. Please stop! It Mr. Clark said. Then Lopez replied beg me old man like you made my brother beg you that morning.

Mr. Clark said oh yea, I can't wait until the both of you brats are in there with your brother. Why do you think we are having so much fun breaking your windows old man? Then Pedro said Lopez mama is going to be angry with us. Then Lopez said I don't care. I want to be with Nick, Pedro.

Then Mr. Clark yelled and said to Lopez, the police are on their way here, you little brats. Are you sure Mr. Clark do I have enough time to break out one more window in your car? As Lopez picked up another rock, before he could throw the rock the police pulled up and asked Lopez and Pedro what was going on.

Lopez replied and told the police that he didn't like Mr. Clark. So I just broke his windows out. Then the officer put Lopez and Pedro in the back seat of the police car. Mr. Clark walked over to talk to the police officer. Lopez had his window down and was making smart remarks at Mr. Clark.

Saying oh Mr. Policeman where can I get some new windows at, as you can see mine are broken. Then Lopez noticed that the people that were standing around and started laughing every time Lopez would say something. Then Lopez said no one would happen to have an extra windshield in their garage at home. Because if it rains I don't believe they make an umbrella big enough to cover my car on the way home.

Everybody started laughing again, including the police officer. Then Mr. Clark really got angry. The officer looked at Mr. Clark and replied, sir you will have to come down to the station and file charges. Later back at the store everyone was working. An unexpected call came in on the phone.

Maria answered it, and then looked around to see where Eldora was. So that Eldora couldn't hear her conversation.

CHAPTER 10

MARIA THEN WENT TO the stock room to talk to George. Maria said to George we have a real problem. Lopez and Pedro are in trouble for breaking Mr. Clark store windows out, and they have both of the boys down at the police station. Then George replied, you didn't say anything to Eldora did you.

No George I didn't I was afraid to said Maria. That's why I came back here; I wanted to tell you dear. Listen to me Maria; keep Eldora busy while I run down to the police station. I have to get them boys home before Eldora finds out about this, said George.

As George left to go the police station, when he got there, the two boys were sitting down being questioned by the officer. Mr. Clark was complaining, saying to the boys if you little brats were my kids, Then George got angry and looked at Mr. Clark and said. Well there not your kids, and I would appreciate if you wouldn't call them little brats, and if you disrespect my boys one more time, I will give you a whooping your father never gave you.

Then George over heard Lopez telling Pedro, Mr. Conner's really does love us. Then George looked at the officer and said, how much are the damages, the officer replied the estimate are around two thousand four hundred and twenty-four dollars, Will that be cash or check said George.

Then Lopez and Pedro got up from their seats and walked over to George. Lopez said to Mr. Conner I appreciate you being here for me and my brother.

I also appreciate what you said. Now I know that you love us, and we are proud of you. But please understand that me and Pedro want to go and be with Nick. Mr. Conner's please don't pay Mr. Clark. Let us go because we don't belong here.

We are tired of kids making fun of us. What do I tell your mother Lopez, said George? Tell her we will always love her and she knows how we feel about Nick. We know that you and Mrs. Conner will take care of her, said Lopez.

Boys what is I suppose to do, when I can't see you guys anymore. I will miss you said George. Then Lopez looked at George and said you can come see us anytime you want. I love you papa, Pedro replies I love you to papa. I love you my sons replied George.

The officer said to George, I guess the little guys made up their minds sir. Then George asked the officer what is going to happen next. The officer replied, as he looked at George, the boys will be placed together in a holding cell until nine o'clock in the morning. The judge will have a speedy trial; he is going on a long vacation and won't be back until a day before Christmas.

The boys will be sent off to the correctional center tomorrow, it's according how they plea to the judge. George asked the officer do you have decent blankets to keep the boys warm tonight. George was getting upset, the officer replied sir please don't get upset.

This place is not an animal shelter, when it comes to children they get special treatment. I couldn't help to overhear the conversation between you and the boys. They committed a crime just to be with their brother, and I thought about my son at home. It bothers me to sir.

George asked can I take the boys out long enough to get them something to eat; they haven't had anything to eat since early this morning.

The officer replied, I'm sorry but we can't allowed that, but I'll tell you what we can do sir. Why don't you ask the boys what they want to eat, and you can go out and get what they want, and bring it back to them. We have a lobby in the back, and you can sit with them while they eat.

All we ask is that you don't buy any kind of metal container or glass. While you all are back there, there is an eleven year old boy in a cell on the left, don't talk to him. He had murdered his seven year old brother. Then George replied "oh god."

How did he kill his brother, then the officer said, he put his brother in a freezer and the little boy suffocated to death. I'm not having my boys back there with a killer. The officer replied, your boys will be protected, I promise you, and sir please hurry and get your boys something to eat because visiting hours will be over soon and you'll have to leave.

George asked the boys what they wanted to eat. George left quickly, and while George was gone, the officer said would you boys like to go in the back to the lobby and wait on your papa.

The boys said, that will be OK, the officer said follow me. The officer opens the jail entrance door as the boys past the jail cell they heard someone crying. Lopez and Pedro looked to their left, and they saw the boy sitting on his bunk bed with his elbows on his knees, his hands over his eyes crying.

Then the boy raised his head up, looking at Lopez and Pedro. It frightens them because the boy had a bad scar on his left jaw. How he looked, he had swollen eyes from where he was crying so much, his hair was very dirty. The officer told the boys don't look at him, because he has enough problems. Then Lopez and Pedro went and sat down, Lopez looked at the officer and said. What happened to his jaw, he told us that he fell on a broken bottle when he was younger, replied the officer.

The officer said, listen I've got to step out for a few minutes will you boys be OK, I'll leave the main door open, then Lopez said we will be fine. As Lopez and Pedro was sitting down, Pedro looked at Lopez and said, I feel bad for that little kid Lopez, I do to Pedro, said Lopez then Lopez said, this place looks better than our bedroom, I know and we got separate beds to, said Pedro.

Then George came rushing in bringing new pillows and new blankets. And he said I'm sorry if I took so long, but I went to a store and bought you boys something to keep you both warm, and I got you guys some comic books to read and I got to go back to the car and get you guy's your favorite foods, then George left again, and came back quickly, bringing Lopez his big box of pizza and Pedro his most favorite treats, a bag full of taco's, then George said, I've got another bag here for my boy's, Pedro said what, well said George I've got all kind of cakes, candy, and a bunch of soda pop in plastic bottles, and this way I won't have to worry about you boys not having anything to eat tonight, how come you're not eating with us, said Lopez. I'm too upset to eat right now, why don't you boy's let me pay Mr. Clark so I can take you home with me.

I will buy you anything you want, like a new bicycle or toys or games anything, just come home please, George was getting upset again and he said, I don't want you boy's to stay in this dark and dreary place. Can you guys understand that, then Lopez said papa it's not bad here, me and Pedro said earlier this place looked better than our bedroom at home, and here we got our own beds.

And the policemen are nice to us, and here no one makes fun of us, then the officer said visiting hours are up, then George put his arms around both of the boy's Pedro said papa why are you holding us so tight. Because I don't want to let you go, George said to them I will always love you boys, and I will be here early in the morning for your hearing then George left, and got in his car and shut the door.

And looked around and slowly laid his head on the steering wheel, and started crying. And when George came to his senses he didn't know what to tell Eldora, and when he got back to the store, as he walked through the door, he tried to avoid looking at Eldora, he motioned for Maria to step in the stock room with him, while George was telling Maria everything that happened between the boy's and Mr. Clark and the police.

Eldora felt something was wrong, she locked the front door to go and see what was going on, mean while George said to Maria, I don't know how to tell her Maria, then Maria looked at George and said, look at me my husband, I didn't only married you because I only love you, I also married you because there's never was a problem to small or too big for you to handle.

Or a mountain to high, for you to climb, or a bridge to narrow for you to cross, George you've always had answers for problems, and you will find an answer for this one. So as George and Maria walked out of the stock room, they met Eldora half way. Eldora looked at George and said George what's wrong? because I can see it in your eyes that you are upset, and then George said.

Eldora please sit down, because I need to talk to you, after George and Eldora talked either though, Eldora was upset and crying she looked at George and said, I've never been so upset, but talking to you I feel a comfort so strong George I need to go home and lay down and sleep, then George said it's almost closing time Eldora, let's go on and close up and go to my house.

And I can keep an eye on you, thank- you said, Eldora then Maria whispered to George, I told you that you would find an answer for this problem, no said George god had an answer, then they left the store and went home. Mean while back at the police station, Lopez and Pedro was in their cell block with the door open, and an officer walked in and looked at them and said would you boys like to come with me and watch some television. They said no sir but thank-you, we like our beds that we are laying on, they may be hard, but they are not like our beds at home

At least, with sharp springs sticking out of them, then the officer said I'll have extra pads added later before you boy's go to bed, and I'll leave the door unlocked till eight o'clock, if you need to use the restroom just yell and I will unlock the door for you, me and my fellow officer already know the story about you boy's.

What he did to your brother, and we don't like Mr. Clark either. Then Lopez replied sir would you like some pizza, taco, or soda pop. No thank- you son, but that's kind of you said the officer. I'll see you later. As the officer walked out the little boy in the other jail cell said, sir I'll watch the television with you. The officer got very hateful with the little boy and replied no you'll never watch television in my station.

As Lopez and Pedro was laying in their beds reading there comic books, a few minutes later the little boy said my name is Roman, I've been here for nine days. It gets lonely in here, I'm hungry and thirsty, and I get cold at nights. Then Lopez looked at Pedro and whispered, we're not allowed to talk to him. Then the little boy said please talk to me.

The only thing I had to eat today was two biscuits and a slice of bacon. I heard you when you asked the police officer if he wanted anything, I wouldn't ask for anything if I wasn't so hungry. Then Pedro said Lopez, he might really be hungry and mama always had an answer for everything. If she was here she would probably look at you Lopez and say. Does god not feed the birds in the air?

Pedro walked over to Roman's cell block and introduced themselves. Lopez asked Roman why you are hungry, don't they feed you in here. They do said Roman, but there was this big bully in here with me, and he would make me give my food to him or he would beat me up. What would you like to eat, replied Lopez. We have pizza, tacos, cakes, and soda pop.

CHAPTER 11

ANYTHING REPLIED THE BOY, Lopez went back to his cell and got some pizzas, soda pop and a cake and went to Roman's cell. As Lopez was turning the pizza box side ways to put it through the bars, Roman quickly grabbed it out of Lopez hands. He accidentally spilled the pizza on the floor; Pedro looked at Roman and said how you can eat that pizza when it fell on the floor.

Roman didn't answer Pedro. Lopez whispered to Pedro, he is so hungry, that he is eating like an animal. Lopez said lets go back to our room Pedro. When the boys got back to their room, Pedro said Lopez I thank god I'm never been that hungry. Can I take two tacos to him; Lopez said yes you can Pedro.

Pedro got two tacos and went to Roman cell. Pedro stood on the outside looking in at Roman licking the sauce out of the pizza box, and then Pedro replied, Roman would you like to have these two tacos. Oh yes, replied Roman. This is the best I've ate since I've been in here, no this is the best I've ate in months, thank-you so much Pedro.

Lopez steps out of his cell, and said Pedro get back here it sounds like somebody is coming. Then Pedro went back to his cell and sat on his bed, and the officer walked in and replied boys it's about time to close and lock the doors. Do you boys want your door locked or left opened? So you two can go into the lobby during the night and use the rest rooms. Lopez and Pedro replied, leave it unlock sir, thank-you. Then the officer locked the main door and left.

Roman replied, Lopez and Pedro I want to thank-you so much for the food, you guys gave me. You all are real friends; you all are the only friends I have.

Listen guys, the policeman won't be in here for the rest of the night, unless someone asks for them. Please come back here and talk to me. Lopez replied to Roman, since it is getting a little bit late, let me and my brother say our nightly prayers and after we get done we'll be down to talk to you, OK said Roman.

When the boys got done praying, they went back down to Roman's cell to talk with him. Roman looked at Lopez and said, I can barely see you guys out of the corner of my eye from here, and if you don't mind my asking, why were you and your brother down on your knees and who were you talking to.

Lopez said to Roman we were praying to god our creator. Do you know god Roman. No I don't, but please tell me about him. I have nothing but time. I've been told that I will serve in the boy's correctional center until I'm eighteen. I will have to go to prison for a very long time, please if you don't mind, please tell me about your god.

For the next hour and a half Lopez and Roman were talking about god when Lopez got done, Roman looked at Lopez and said, thank you for helping me to find hope. Roman put his right hand through the bar and laid it on Lopez right shoulder and said, Lopez my friend will you kneel and pray with me. I will be glad to pray with you said Lopez. As they were praying Roman started crying with tears of joy.

When they got done praying Roman looked at Lopez and replied, Lopez I've never felt so much joy in my life. Thank- you for letting me know about Jesus. I know now when I die I will get to be with my brother Antonio again. Lopez said to Roman, now can I ask you a question. Without you getting angry, I won't get angry with you Lopez, go ahead and ask me said Roman.

Why would you want to be with you brother when you killed him.

Lopez my friend, I am glad you asked me that question, but first your brother Pedro looks very tired. Please let him go on to bed. And another favor before you lay down tonight, do you have an extra blanket that I can borrow, it gets cold during the night.

I will bring you a blanket I promise. Roman said Lopez, that question you asked me earlier, now we can talk since Pedro went to bed. What I'm about to tell you my friend, must remain a secret. Can you keep a promise when I tell you, yes I can replied Lopez.

I didn't kill my brother; let me tell you what really happened Lopez. Less than two years ago, my father was on his way home from work and was killed in an auto accident. Antonio was five years old, and I was ten. My mother started going to the bars and getting drunk. One night she brought a man home with her; at first he was nice to us. He would take us to the parks, sometimes to the movies.

Then my mother and he got married, and then shortly after that, he changed. He started picking on Antonio a lot. One night I told him to leave my brother alone. Then he took his belt off, and turned it around and hit me with the belt buckle. It cut my face, that's how I got the scar on my face. My mother took me to the hospital, my step father told me to tell them I fell on a broken glass bottle or he would kill me.

My brother and I would live in fear everyday with him. My mother wasn't only getting drunk; she was also doing drugs to. My stepfather was constantly beating on Antonio. Then one night, I was in my room and Antonio was in his room, earlier that evening. He told Antonio to take out the trash, I told my step father to let me do it because it was too heavy for my brother to take it out. He accidentally spilled the garbage down the steps.

My step father waited until that night to punish him. Roman got very emotional. Back to that night, I said earlier when I was in my room, and Antonio was in his, I heard my step father walk in my brothers room and he said to Antonio. This is for not being able to carry your weight around the house.

Roman started crying, and said, Lopez I'll never forget the sound of my baby brother voice begging my step father to stop beating him. I felt so helpless that night. When he got done beating Antonio, I heard my step father slam the door, when he walked out of his room. I was sitting on the edge of the bed scared to death.

I didn't know what to do. When I heard Antonio crying, and saying please bubby, I'm hurting, please help me. So I snuck out of my room very quietly and went into Antonio room. I said to Antonio you must quit crying, or he'll get back up. I can't help it bubby, my back is hurting me said Antonio.

I said to Antonio, let me check your back, I pulled Antonio shirt up. I saw the whelps and bruises; Antonio said my back is killing me. I will go and see where he is at, then I will bring back some cold rags and put them on your back, OK Antonio said Roman.

As I walked out of the bedroom into the hallway, I checked my mother's room and my step father wasn't there. Then I quietly walked down the steps to the living room there he was passed out drunk on the couch, with the belt in his hand. So I went back upstairs to the bathroom, and I got some washcloths and ran cold water on them, and went back to Antonio room. I laid the cold rags on his back; he said bubby that makes my back feel better. But why does our step father hate us so much.

Lopez looked at Roman and said I have sat here and listen to you for a long time, but why didn't you go to the police, neighbors or even tell the school teacher what was going on. They would have put him in jail Roman.

Roman replied, listen Lopez my friend, we couldn't tell any teachers because when he put any marks on us, he would keep us home from school, until the wounds would heal. We couldn't tell the neighbors because we weren't allowed outside to play. He kept us inside the house, and how could we tell the police when we wasn't allowed to use the phone.

He kept the phone locked up in his room, and my mother would lie for him if we would have told the law the truth, because she needed the drugs he was giving to her.

Then one night I decided I had to do something or he was going to kill me or my brother. So I got a couple of garbage bags and I put some pillows and blankets in the bags. I got me and Antonio some clothes and stuff in the bags also.

Then I waited one night until my step father and mother went to sleep. I got Antonio out of bed, and then we snuck out of the house. We got half way through town, and I found a dark alley. And then I noticed some giant boxes, so I got one of them. I got the bed clothes out of the bags, and made a bed inside it. Lopez it was nice and warm inside.

Antonio and I were so happy; we didn't have to worry about getting yelled at or getting beat on. Then I had to learn to steal for food. So during the day we would hide out. Then I would wait until the late evening came and I would put on my hooded sweater. I made Antonio stay in the box until I came back with the food.

I would go to these outside markets and steal apples, bananas, and any kind of food I could get. Everything was going well until one day a heavy rain hit. Our cardboard box got wet, and so did our pillow and blankets even our clothes. I knew I had to find a new hiding place because the rain was pouring down. Antonio and I walked further up to the end of the back alley.

I notice across some railroad tracks there were an old abandon junk yard not far away. After we got there the sign said no trespassing. Then we crawled under the fence, as we walked through the junk yard, I saw an old black car sitting on a cinder blocks.

Antonio and I got in it and rolled up the windows to keep the rain off of us. At this time Roman was telling Lopez the final story of what really happened to his brother. But it was hard for him to tell Lopez without crying.

While me and Antonio was sitting in front seat of the car, Antonio looked over at me and said bubby I'm cold so I reached over and tore off the upholstery on the ceiling of the car and wrapped it around us, to keep us warm, we slept for a long time.

The next morning Antonio woke me up coughing, I said to him, Antonio are you OK, he said to me, bubba I'm sick, then I knew I had to do something, I said listen to me Antonio, I will go into town and get some food, and I will get some medicine, for your cough, and also remember if you see anybody coming hide somewhere else OK. I will yell for you to come out when I come back, then he said, something to me, that I will never forget, he said bubba, let's go back home, please I told him, that our stepfather will kill us, then he looked up at me and said, it doesn't matter. I feel like I'm dying anyhow, I said Antonio you'll be alright just give me a half an hour to forty five minutes and I will be back, you'll be better once you take some cough syrup Antonio, then I left and I ran as fast as I could down town.

I seen a pharmacy store, then I went in, and no one was looking, I grabbed a bottle of cough syrup and ran out, then I noticed there was a hotdog stand on the corner of the street, and while the owner wasn't looking I quickly grabbed a bunch of hotdogs and ran as fast as I could getting back to the junkyard.

CHAPTER 12

I APPROACHED THE CAR, and Antonio wasn't sitting up waiting for me, as I opened the door, he was lying down in the front seat shivering, and I got in, I said Antonio, I have some medicine for you.

I noticed when I raised his head, he was very hot, I held the cough syrup up to his mouth, he took it, then I said I've got some hotdogs Antonio, then he looked at me and said, I'm not hungry bubba, I told him if he wasn't any better, that evening, that I would go back to the drug store.

And get something else for him, I thought for awhile he quit coughing, that he was feeling better, because he started talking to me, then all of a sudden, he got worse, then I said Antonio.

I have to go back to the drug store one more time and get you something better that will help you and I thought stealing was easy until that night, because they were waiting on me to return, but before I left I told Antonio, I had to get him something better.

You know what Lopez, since he was born, I don't remember him even calling me by my name, the very first time before I left him that night, he looked at me and said, I understand why you care so much about me, and because you love me bubba.

Lopez, I'll never forget the way he looked at me, and smiling, that was the last time I saw him alive, and when I went into town late that evening. I walked into the pharmacy store, and asked the pharmacist what kind of medicine I would need for my brothers, symptoms.

I told him that he had a high fever and he wasn't eating and he also was having bad headaches, then the pharmacist went and got me the medicine that I needed and he put them on the counter for me to pay for them.

I knew that I had to move quickly, so I grabbed the medicine and I ran toward the front door, and then there was a security guard waiting for me , he looked at me and said, we seen you earlier today, when you stole some cough syrup, and I said please let me go, because my brother maybe dying sir.

He looked at me and said, it's not my problem tell it to the police, because they are on their way here, when the police arrived they put me in the patrol car and question me I told the truth about everything.

I told them more importantly about my brother how sick he was, and I told them me and my brother were runaways, and who my parents were and my stepfather and my mother didn't even report us even missing so that's how much they cared about me and Antonio.

Then they asked me exactly where my brother was, I told them about the junkyard, so they took me there, and I showed them the car they said to me, stay in the patrol car, while we investigate, and when they came back, they looked at me and said where is he, quit playing games he's not in the car.

I told them to let me out, and all I had to do is yell for him, then they let me out and I began yelling hey Antonio for about forty five seconds then we waited for a couple of minutes, and he never did answer me.

Then I yelled Antonio please come out, from hiding the police are here to help us, and take you to the hospital, then one officer looked at the other officer, and said we better call for help, and get a search party here.

Because it's getting dark, and this is a big junk yard, then the officer said I'll make the call now, just a few minutes later, four squad cars pulled into the junk yard, the officer looked at me and said, son stay in the back of the patrol car.

We'll let you know if we find your brother or not, I watched ten or eleven policemen, go into the junk yard with their flashlight and their k-9 dogs, and while they were gone, I was trying to figure out, why Antonio would not answer me, and why he would leave the car.

Unless he seen someone coming, while I was gone then a few seconds later, I seen a stranger with a flashlight, shining it at the other patrol car, then he shined his light on me then he walked over to the patrol car, that I was in he tapped his flashlight, on my window .

But I couldn't roll it down, but the front driver side window was down he lowered his head and said to me son do you know what's going on here, I said to him they are looking for my brother sir, then the stranger said, earlier I was walking though here. And I watched a little boy get out of that black car, over there.

I guess I frighten him, because he ran into the back of the junk yard, I didn't mean no harm, see I'm the watchman for this junk yard, but I yelled for him to come to me, but he didn't listen to me, then I noticed another flashlight.

Shining my way, only one policeman came back he quickly got in the car and he got on his radio, and said we need an ambulance at the old abandon junk yard, on the east side as soon as possible.

And after he got done talking, I said where is my bother at sir, he didn't answer me, he got out of the car and open my door, and said to me get out of the car and follow me, on the way to the back of the junk yard.

I kept asking him where's my brother, why didn't you just get him, so we can take him to the hospital, he still wouldn't answer me, Lopez then it hit me when we got there, I seen all the policemen gathered around Antonio, laying on the ground.

And one of the officers was giving him CPR, then I looked up and there was a chest type freezer with the lid open, then I knew what happened, to my brother that night, he got scared and got in the freezer and suffocated, to death.

As I was standing there looking at Antonio, I will never forget when I was looking at his face, it had a shade of blue and he looked so helpless, the officer said to me. I'm sorry for not answering any of your questions.

I need you to make a positive identification, now I have to ask you is this your brother, Lopez I was so shocked, that I couldn't remember any of the questions, he asked me and that was when he said, I'm taking you back to the station, we will have to file a report.

And since you are a runaway, we will have to contact your parents, and let them take you home, and when we got back to the station, he did his report and then he called my stepfather and my mother and told them to come down to the police station.

And after he got off the phone, I said sir, please let me sit with you when they get here, he said to me just call me Mr. Johnson, and yes you can sit with me, then he looked at me and said is there something you should be telling me.

I just looked at him and said please don't make me go home with them, please then my mother and stepfather came, rushing into the police station asking the officer what happened, officer Johnson looked at her and said, there's been a bad accident.

I'd would like for you and your husband, and son to step into our private room, we'll sit at the table and discuss what has happened, Lopez as we were sitting there, the detective told her what has happened then the detective said I know you're upset.

But I need to ask you some questions, about things I don't understand, can you and your husband answer them for me, my mother said. I will try to answer them the best way, I can, go ahead and ask me sir.

Lopez, what my mother said next, shocked me she told nothing but lies, on me, when the detective asked her how did her son get bruises on his back, and his legs when they found him, and how come you didn't report your son's running away.

Then my mother said, I can answer those questions for you, Mr. Johnson see Roman has a bad temper, he was always beating on his brother, and when my husband would tried to correct him he would threaten him, he told me that he was going to take Antonio and run away.

And if I called the law on him, and when he got out of jail that he would kill us both, after all, look what he did to Antonio, I can't forgive him for what he did to my baby, me and my husband don't feel safe around him, then my mother started fake crying, and she said can we go now.

I don't want to look at him, then the detective said yes you may go now, I'm sorry for your loss and if I need any more information, I will get in contact with you, then after they left the detective sat down with me and said look at me Roman, is this true everything they said.

I didn't answer him, Lopez because I was sitting there thinking, how my mother didn't show any real emotions, then I thought when they came to the police station that I would have to go home, with them.

I would rather take the blame, for my brother's death then to take another beaten. Like Antonio did then, I realized the detective was still talking to me, saying please Roman talk to me.

Because this is a serious crime you can be put to death, for this you are a young boy, and I just trying to help you, tell me the truth before it's too late I still didn't answer him, when he mentioned death to me I thought of Antonio.

The only thing I did loved is gone, and everything else doesn't matter, to me anymore, and it didn't matter what I said no one would have believed me, that I didn't do it, then the detective said, I have no choice.

But to charge you with murder, since you won't answer me, and then they put me here, if you don't mind Lopez, let me show you a picture, of me and my brother, this was taken a year before my father died.

That's me holding Antonio, by the Christmas tree, see how happy we where, together this is the only memory I have of him Lopez, since I listen to you, said Lopez I want you to listen to me now, my papa is a very rich man, he can get you a very good lawyer,.

To get you out of this trouble and it's not too late, we can put your stepfather in jail, and your mother too if you want, my mother will give you a good home, she will love you just like she loves me and my brothers.

And your brother is in a better place, and one day you will see him again Roman, then Roman said, there's not an hour or a minute that goes by, that I don't think of him, I can't wait till that day, that I'll get to be with him again.

Lopez my friend, I'm not afraid to die, I hope they will put me to death soon, I want to live in this place you call heaven, I appreciate you offering me a new home, but please understand me, I want to be with my brother, Lopez and I want you to make me a promise, please Lopez don't tell anyone what I have told you.

You must keep this promise, you're the only friend that I have and trust you, now can you keep this promise my friend, I promise said Lopez, and I will go and get you that blanket for you now.

And when Lopez returned, Roman said to him, my special friend don't look so depressed, since I met you, you gave me hope and help me find, peace and joy just knowing you are here gives me comfort.

I've never felt so tired and sleepy, thank-you Lopez, I'll see you in the morning my friend, Lopez smiled and said goodnight Roman, then Lopez returned to his cell to check on Pedro, Lopez got on his knees and said a special prayer for Roman.

Then he said Jesus watch over my brother, and never take one of them away from me, please, I love you lord, Amen, as the morning came and the officer opened the main doors, and yelled boys it's time for all of you to wake up.

Because all of you got to go to court this morning, so eat your breakfast and try to look decent as they brought the food trays in, Lopez heard the cook asking Roman how that pizza box got in your cell.

Roman wouldn't answer, then the cook said, since you won't answer me, I'll just take your tray back, as the cook turned around to leave, Lopez was standing in the way, and said to the cook, either you give him his food tray, or I will give him mine, or when I go to court this morning, I will tell my papa that you wouldn't Feed me.

CHAPTER 13

THE COOK SAID TO Lopez, don't you realized that he killed his own brother, what's the different, you're trying to starve him to death, then the cook left, Roman said to Lopez thank-you Lopez, Lopez said don't mention it,

Then he went back to his cell to eat with Pedro, as Lopez and Pedro were sitting there after they got done eating, Lopez said to Pedro I got a feeling, when we go to court this morning.

Papa is going to try to pay Mr. Clark for his windows and take us home Pedro, what are we going to do about it, I want to go and be with Nick, OK. Little brother said Lopez, I got a plan this is what's going too happened, only three of us are going to court.

This morning me and you and Roman, Pedro do you remember the story mama use to tell us, about David and the giant, yes I remember, said Pedro and then Lopez said, do you remember how you use to wrestle with us, and you would jump on Nick's back, and he couldn't get you off.

What are you getting at Lopez, said Pedro comes here and I will whisper it to you, because I don't want Roman to hear us, after Lopez and Pedro got done whispering to each other.

Lopez said to Pedro remember we will only do this, if worst comes to worst little brother, sounds like fun to me. Said Pedro then a couple minutes later an officer opened the main door, and came in and said, are my little criminals ready to go to court this morning.

They unlocked Romans cell, and put handcuff's on him and the three boys' went out of the station, and got in the back of the squad car, Roman said to Lopez I am nervous and scared, going to court knowing that my stepfather, is going to be there.

That night a detective name Mr. Johnson protected me from him, at the police station don't worry Roman, me and Pedro got your back, then Lopez and Pedro grinned at each other, when they arrived at the court house, the boys got out.

Lopez and Pedro got out of the squad car, the two brothers seen Mr. and Mrs. Connors and their mama, they run up to their mother and hugged her, and George and Maria then Eldora looked at Lopez and Pedro said, why are you boys doing this to me, listen to me Lopez and Pedro.

Mr. Connors is going to pay Mr. Clark for the windows and after court you boy's are going home with me, then Lopez looked at his mama and said please mama will you understand me, if I try to explain something to you.

The reason me and Pedro broke out Mr. Clark's window's was that I want to be sent to that place, because I am the only one that can talk to Nick into coming back home, so we can be a family again until he's with us.

Please let us go you'll be alright with the Connors they will take good care of you. Remember mama what god said to you, there's a reason to all things and mama I promise I'll write you every day, so you can understand how much I love my brother.

But if you and Pedro leave me, I can't promise I'll be waiting for you boy's to come back, home because I don't know how much more I can take, then George and Maria walked up to Eldora and the boy's, and the court clerk said, it's almost time for the court hearing to start.

Then the Connors and Eldora and the boy's went in and sat down, in the back row Lopez noticed that Roman was upset and been crying, then George looked over at Eldora and Maria and said theirs that little boy that killed his little brother, as George turned his head and looked around.

Lopez gave George a strange look, and then turned his head then the bailiff said, please stand and rise the honorable judge Manuel, then the judge sat down and said everyone may be seated.

Then the bailiff called out, may the case of Lopez and Pedro Santos please approach the bench, George's attorney that he'd hired to defend Lopez and Pedro walked up in front of the judge, then the attorney said your honor we would like to have the charges dismissed against Lopez and Pedro Santos.

Because this is their first defense sir, and Mr. Connors is willing to pay for all of the damages that was done to Mr. Clark's shoe store, and his car. The judge said has Mr. Connors make out a check to the court for the sum of two thousand and two hundred and twenty four dollars and the case will be dismissed.

And for you two boy's if I ever see you two back in my court room I will send you both to the correctional center for boy's, then the lawyer and the boy's went back and sat down, the lawyer told George that he had one more case, then Eldora could take the boy's home.

As they were sitting there waiting for the lawyer, to get done with his next case, the bailiff called out, will the parents of Roman Gabriel please approach the bench, the attorney looked at the judge, and said your honor my client has plead guilty to the charge of murder for the death of his brother.

He is now awaiting sentencing then the judge looked at Roman, and said young man do you have anything to say before I pass sentence on you, no your honor all I ask can you have me put to death, so when I see my brother, I can tell him I'm sorry.

No said the judge I am going to have you stay at the correctional center for boy's until you are Eighteen then from their you'll spend most of your life in the Texas state Prison, you'll have plenty of time to think about what you have done to your brother.

Then the judge looked at Romans parent's and said do either one of you have anything to say to your son before I send him away, yes your honor, said the mother, she looked at Roman and said I hope you rot in prison. Mean while Lopez was listening to what she was saying to Roman.

Then George noticed Lopez was getting upset, he looked down at Lopez and replied, what's wrong Lopez tells me I can't tell you because I made a promise papa, said Lopez.

It got so bad, that Lopez couldn't handle it any longer, the way the both of them were talking to Roman standing there with his head hanging down, and watching his tears hitting the floor, then Lopez whispered to Pedro and said do you remember back in the jail cell, what we whispered about.

And there's only one officer in the courtroom, and also do you remember when I said only if worst comes to worst then Lopez said to Pedro, little brother are you ready to wrestle, oh yea said, Pedro let's do it now, said Lopez.

Lopez and Pedro leaped over the bench; Pedro ran and jumped on the officer's back the officer ran around in a circle trying to get Pedro off of his back, the judge pounding his mallet on his desk yelling order in the court.

Lopez ran towards the judge's desk and grabbed the mallet out of the judge's hand and quickly went up to Roman stepfather, and hit him in the side of the face with it then he fell down on his back, then Lopez started kicking and stomping him.

And sat on his chest and whispered in his ear, that's for Antonio several more officers rushed in the courtroom, to help get Pedro off the officer back, and grabbed Lopez off of Roman's stepfather. The judge said please get my mallet back. So I can restore order, once order was restored the judge told the officers, to handcuff the two brothers, and bring them back to the bench, he looked at Lopez and Pedro, and said I gave you boy's a chance, to better yourselves now I'm taking back that chance.

Because the disturbance that you two caused, in my courtroom, I have no choice but to send you two to the correctional center for boys, then Lopez and Pedro smiled at each other because they knew that they got their wish.

Meanwhile George and Maria was comforting Eldora, from all of the excitement, and Roman's mother was giving her husband medical attention, Lopez and Pedro was standing with Roman, the three boys were whispering to each other.

Lopez was looking in the front row at Roman's stepfather laughing at him, Roman said to Lopez what are you doing Lopez, don't worry Roman said Lopez I kept my promise, I didn't say nothing.

But I didn't promise I wouldn't do anything about it, then Lopez looked at Pedro and said out loud, oh look at that poor man, he got a big knot on the side of his face, then Pedro laughed Roman's stepfather got angry.

And got up out of his seat and started walking towards George, Romans mother looked at him and said don't start any trouble James and then he looked at George, and said Mister I would appreciate if you would do something with your boy's sir.

I don't mean no disrespect, but if you got a problem with my boy's, I would be glad for me and you to step out back of the court house where no one can see us, and I will solve your problem for you.

Then Roman's parent's just walked away, George walked to one of the officer's, and said can I talk to the boy's before they leave, sorry sir said the officer you'll have to wait and see them in the correctional center or wait till they contact you by mail.

Then George and Maria and Eldora waved at the boy's as they went out of the doors, then the Connors and Eldora got in George's car and left to go back home.

Maria turned around to look at Eldora and said are you upset Eldora, no said Eldora for some strange reason I believe Lopez when he said that he will bring Nick home, I am leaving it in god's hands for now on.

That's the spirit, said Maria mean while back in the squad car, Lopez and Pedro and Roman were in the back seat on their way to the correctional center, Roman said, Antonio would had been so proud of you Lopez.

My stepfather was a coward, he wouldn't face your father, you are a true friend Lopez, I feel safe having you around, then Pedro said, I wonder if that is going to leave a scar on your stepfather's face I thought that was funny.

I did to, said Roman, but when my father was alive he use to tell me to stand up for myself, but how are you suppose to stand up against a man like my stepfather, try reading about David and the giant sometimes said Lopez.

Will you read it to me sometimes Lopez, will it help me to be brave, like you and Pedro and why would you and Pedro do that in the courtroom, when you guys had a chance to go home, said Roman.

It's a long story Roman I have a brother at this place we're going to, and his name is Nick, he's our oldest brother, I want to talk him into coming home, as the boy's were on their way to the correctional center.

Lopez told Roman, what had happened, why Nick got in trouble after Lopez told Roman everything. Roman said, so Nick blames his mother for something that wasn't her fault, I can't understand that, but I do understand one thing you and your brother's are close just like me and Antonio was.

I wish I could go and get my brother, and bring him home but I don't have a home to bring him to, Lopez whispered to Roman, and said, listen to me Roman you will see your brother, in a better place one day.

I promise, but you'll have a home to come to, don't you realize you're going to spend most of your life in prison, for something you didn't do, let my papa get you a lawyer, that can help you do you remember our promise Lopez, replied Roman.

I want to be with my brother, just like you want to be with yours, then Lopez said, what are you talking about Roman you're young it will be a long time before you ever get to see your brother.

CHAPTER 14

THEN ROMAN SAID, YOU will know when the time comes, and then you can tell anybody, still Lopez, didn't understand what Roman was talking about. Then the driving officer stopped the car, and he said

Boy's welcome to your new home, they all got out of the car then the officer said follows me to the office.

So I can turn in all your paper work, then the officer said, I pick a good time coming today, because it's lunch time listen boy's let me take off your handcuff's and you all wait out here, in the hallway, I will go in the office, they will send out a guard.

To show you boy's your room, as the boy's were standing in the hallway, waiting for the guard to come, some of the kid's were coming down the hallway, from lunch then Roman got behind Lopez, then Lopez said, what's wrong with you Roman, then Roman said there's that bully that was in my cell.

He would take my food away from me, oh no said Pedro, get ready David because here coma's Goliath then the bully and some of his friend's walked up to Lopez, Pedro, and Roman and said hey Roman have you killed anybody lately.

Then the bully and his friend started laughing, then Lopez said lay off of him I asked you a question, said the bully if you are protecting him who's going to protect you, then Lopez started smiling looking past the bullies shoulder.

And said, my big brother, is going to protect me then the bully turned around, and Nick was standing there Nick looked at the bully and said now, can I ask you a question who's going to protect you Chi co.

Then Nick pushed him down, then Chi co said I'm sorry Nick I didn't know these guys were your brother's, Nick looked at Chi co and said, Chi co spread the word if I ever catch you or anyone in this compound, disrespecting my brother's.

They will suffer my raft, I swear to you now get out of here, Chi co and his friend's quickly walked away, then Nick looked at Lopez and Pedro and said, why are you guys in here, what did you all do, Lopez said, we wanted to prove that we still love you.

I didn't say you guys didn't love me, I said you guy's betrayed me, now what did you and Pedro do, said Nick, then the guard's come back from lunch, and said I'm sorry for taking so long. I just got done having lunch.

Let me show you boy's to your room and read the rules to you boy's, that you all will have to obey, then Nick said to the guard I want to transfer from my room to theirs, because these two are my brother's who's the fourth said the guard.

He's coming with us, said Lopez OK only four are allowed to a room said the guard, and then the guard show the boy's to their rooms. Then the guard left then Nick said to Lopez, now finish telling me what we were talking about early.

Did that old woman turn you and Pedro in, like she did me Lopez said that old woman, is my mother and as long as I'm here don't you ever say that again, OK, Lopez said Nick, just start from the beginning what did you boy's do.

That got you and Pedro in trouble and how did you meet this guy, Roman as Nick and his brother and Roman were sitting in their room just talking about everything, that happened and Nick laughing when Lopez and Pedro told him what happened in court.

They spent the next hour and a half just having a good time, and when they got done Nick said listen Lopez, and Pedro give it up I'll never go back home, oh yes you will my brother, because me and Pedro been praying for a long time said Lopez.

Hey Lopez, said Nick I don't want to talk about this right now OK, but you guys want to have some fun, oh yea, said Pedro, then Nick said some days we get to go swimming, and play football, and baseball, and we also have a medical center and a chapel.

Today they are playing basketball, ready let's go and play, Nick and his brother's went and played basketball, and when they got done, playing in the gym Roman was staring at the basketball goal, Lopez looked back at Roman and said, what are you doing Roman.

Let's go back to our room, then Roman said Lopez how high are these basketball goal's, I say about ten feet, why, said Lopez, Roman said watch this Lopez. Roman quickly climbs all the way up to the top of the goal, and said Lopez I can see Nick and Pedro walking back into our room from here.

Then Lopez said hurry back down Roman before you get caught, I don't want you to get in any kind of trouble, then Roman came down, and he and Lopez walked back to the room.

After they went back to the room, Nick said, it's almost dinner time soon listen I have enough time to go to my old room, and move my things over here, to my new closet Nick left and came back fifteen minutes later,

Bringing clothes and two shoe boxes back with him, as Nick was hanging up his clothes, he said look here guy's I made most of my own clothes, that's what I like about this place they teach you about anything you want to learn to do.

I learned to make my own outfits, then Nick said, hand me those shoe boxes, Pedro, as Pedro got ready to hand the shoe boxes to Nick, he accidentally dropped them both on the floor, and when they hit the floor hard, the lid of the boxes flew off.

A whole bunch of letter's fell out of both boxes, then Pedro said wow Nick, I didn't know that you had so many friends, to write you, he don't said Lopez, just leave them there, I'll put them back in the boxes said Nick.

Lopez disregarded what Nick said, as Lopez was helping Pedro, putting the letter's back in the boxes, Lopez noticed all of the letters were from his mother. And all of them were still sealed. And none were never open, Lopez looked at Nick and said why are you saving these letter's, if you are not going to read them, then Nick said because one day, when I get out of here I want to pay her one more visit I didn't need her to write me and give her all her letter's back to her.

Then Roman said, I know it's none of my business, but I wish I had a mother like her, because Lopez told me everything, about your mother, I wish I had a mother that wanted me home, Lopez you were there in court and heard my mother say that she hope's I rot in jail.

I would love for my mother to tuck me in bed at night, when me and my brother would go to bed at night, all we had to look forward to was a beating from my stepfather, almost every night, you all had a nice warm house to live in.

And a hot meal to eat, in my last days before coming here, me and Antonio had to live in a cardboard box, and a junk car at this time Nick, was still putting his closet in order, but at the same time listening to every word, Roman was saying.

Then Nick said, how did you get food and how did you get here, then Roman gave Lopez a strange look, while Nick wasn't looking then Roman said I would steal food during the day for me and my brother.

And finally I got caught stealing and the law sent me here, where is your bother at, said Nick, then Roman said, someone told me that he lived in a mansion. Then he smiled at Lopez, oh that's good said Nick.

When I stole food I had to do it because me and my brother had to survive, and why would you steal a pair of shoes for your brother, when your mother would have gotten him a pair, sooner or later and why would you blame your mother for putting you in here.

When it's the store owner's fault, not your mother's, then Nick got very angry and turned around and walked toward Roman, and pushed him against the wall, choking Roman, with his hands and he said to Roman you're right Roman.

It's none of your business, then Lopez quickly tried to pull Nick off of Roman, Nick was so out of it, Lopez took his fists started punching Nick in his back, and then Pedro said not again, fighting in the courtroom, this morning and now here to.

I don't think so, then Pedro pushed Lopez out of the way, and jumped up on Nick's back, and put his arm around Nick's neck in a choke hold, then Nick got weak and said OK. Pedro stop it, so I can sit down then the boy's finally quit fighting as Lopez was aiding Roman sitting on one bed.

Nick and Pedro was sitting in the other bed, Nick looked at Roman and said, you're lucky, because the only reason I didn't kill you, is because you are my brother's friend, just mind your business and we will get along okay.

Then Roman said, I'm sorry Nick, I'll never mention it again I promise, well listen guy's it's time to go to lunch, then Nick said it's none of my business, Roman but how did you get that scar on the side your face, I fell on a broken bottle when I was little, said Roman.

Then Roman grind at Lopez, then they all went to lunch, as the first week of stay at the center pasted, the brother's and Roman were having a lots of fun, playing sports and swimming all the boy's made new friends, and each of the boy's picked a hobby.

Lopez picked baseball, and started reading about baseball legend's, Pedro picked, wood shop, learning to build little wooden fire trucks and firemen, Roman wanted to learn to be an artist, but things started changing, the second week of stay at the center.

Because when the brother's and Roman, got up one morning and went to breakfasts they got their tray's and went to sit down, at the table with their friend's the brother's and Roman noticed everyone got up from the table, and went to another table.

Just leaving the three brother's and Roman, sitting there by themselves, and after they got done eating they went back to their room, and got dressed to go outside to play baseball, as the boy's walked towards the baseball field, to play with them, the other kid's quit playing and walked off the field.

Nick said, to his brother's and Roman what's going on, everybody act's like they are mad at us, as they went back to the center, as they were walking through the hallway on the way back to the room, their friend's were turn their backs when they would say hi, to them.

After they went in their room's and got situated, Nick said, I got to go to the restroom, Nick noticed Chi co was with five or six of his friend's standing in the hallway staring at him, then Chi co walked up to Nick and said, Nick we need to talk, what about said Nick.

Then Chi co said it's about Roman, everybody here always liked you Nick, and your brother's get to the point Chi co, said Nick, mean while back in the boy's room Lopez said, I wonder where Nick is at, and Roman said I will go and check, as Roman went out of the room and down the hall he saw Chi co and Nick talking.

And hid around the corner, over hearing the conversation then Roman went back to the room, and told Lopez, that Nick was on his way, back to the room.

Then Nick came back, Lopez said, where have you been Nick, just talking to some friend about playing baseball, they wanted you guys to come back out and play, but I said I had something to do first, Lopez and Pedro you two can go out and play.

I want Roman to help me with some boxes down stairs for a few minutes.

And when we get done, we will be out to play, Lopez and Pedro went on out to play, then Nick and Roman went down stairs, Roman noticed that Nick locked the door as they interred the stock room. Nick turned around at Roman and said why did you lie to me, you really didn't need my help did you, said Roman.

I heard you and Chi co talking, are you going to beat me up or kill me down here, neither said Nick, but I was starting to like you, you had me and my brother's believing that you were sent here for stealing, you murdered your own brother.

They don't know that you are a killer, I can't have someone like you around them, but I have a plan there is a hole under the fence and behind the bush, that they don't know about so this is what I want you to do, around twelve o'clock tonight we only have two guard's they both take their lunch break, at the same time this is what I want you to do.

CHAPTER 15

SNEAK OUT THE BACK door, and run as fast as you can, across the field without any one seeing you, where will I go Nick, said Roman, then Nick said that's not for me to worry about, but if you believe in god and if you're not gone by morning, you better be ready to meet him.

Now we are going out to play some baseball, and you will keep your mouth shut, and I will show you were that hole is at, let's go Then Nick and Roman went out to play with the other kids, and when they got done playing, the rest went in and got washed up for dinner except Roman and Nick.

He showed Roman were the hole was at, then they went in and ate, Lopez noticed Roman was quite while he was eating, and was not talking, Lopez said what's wrong with you Roman, then Roman said I'm not feeling well.

I'm going on to our room and lay down while, okay said Lopez, I'll be done shortly and I will check in you, then Roman went to his room, not to lay down, but to write a letter, he got a sheet of his artist paper and started writing.

Sitting on the side of his bed, then the brother's came back from dinner, as they walked into the room, Lopez said to Roman, what are you doing I'm writing a letter to my family, said Roman then Lopez said I thought you weren't close to my family .

Then Roman said, this is to a special family well me and Pedro and Nick are going down stairs, and mess around the shop a little, and if you feel like coming you're welcome, I will understand if you don't because I know that you're not feeling well.

We will be back soon, when the brother's returned, Roman was laying down Lopez noticed Roman's eyes were red, why have you been crying Roman, said Lopez, then Roman said I'm home sick and I miss Antonio so much.

As he whispered to Roman, and how can you be home sick, when you don't have a home said Lopez, get your mind off of that for now, were going down to play some basketball, because it's raining outside, we can't play baseball, then Roman whispered, listen Lopez no one here likes me, and I'm making enemies for you guys I don't want to bring you guys any harm.

Then Nick and Pedro were in the hallway waiting for Lopez to come and play, Nick said come on Lopez, Lopez quickly said Roman remember this, I don't care if any one likes you or me in this place, all that matter is I love you like a brother and you will go home with me someday.

Then Roman said, Lopez I want you to always remember this I love you to because you were the best friend that I ever had, then Lopez left with Nick and Pedro, not realizing that was the last time he would ever see Roman alive.

Nick looked at Lopez and said, what did you and Roman talked about, nothing much he said he was homesick and he missed his brother, and that's about it said Lopez, the brother's went to play basketball and when they got done playing the guard told everybody that it is getting close to Christmas just two and a half weeks away.

That they could help decorate the center, everybody got very happy Lopez said give me a couple of minutes, I want to go and get Roman to help us, then Lopez left to go and get Roman, Lopez walked up to the door and noticed the door was closed he slowly opened the door, he seen Roman down on his knees and praying.

Lopez shut the door quietly, and went back to help with the decorations after everybody got done decorating they returned to their rooms, Lopez and his brothers went into their room, and Lopez checked on Roman, he was already asleep.

The boy's said their prayers and went on to bed, what Lopez didn't know, was that Roman wasn't really sleeping he was just waiting until everybody else to fall asleep, so he could leave. He remembered what Nick said, looking at the clock on the wall to turn twelve o'clock.

The next morning, the boys woke up and got ready for breakfast, without paying attention, Pedro said Lopez where is Roman at. Lopez replied I don't know. Then Lopez walked over to Roman bed and said, why would his pillow and blanket be here but his sheet is gone.

Then Nick said he probably went down to the laundry room to get it washed or to get another one. He's probably taking a shower. This is a big place Lopez, he could be anywhere. Let's go down and eat, I'm hungry; he'll probably be down to eat when he sees, where not there.

The brother's went on down to eat, as the brothers were eating, as Lopez looked at Nick and said, Nick breakfast is almost over and Roman isn't here yet something is not right. Don't worry Lopez, when we get done eating we'll go back to our room. He didn't feel well last night, he probably lay back down.

This time Nick knew he was running out of excuses. When the brothers got done eating they went back to their room. Lopez looked at Nick and said, he's not here Nick where is he at. Nick said Lopez didn't you say last night that he was home sick. I bet he ran away and used the sheet for a cover to sneak out of here.

If Roman ran away said Lopez then why is all his things still in his closet. I'm going to tell the officer and report this. Then Nick said I can't allow you to do that Lopez. There is a rule in here, no one in here, snitch on anyone, it's a rule and we all obey it.

Don't get Roman in trouble if you care about him Lopez. Then Lopez replied where will he go Nick it's pouring down rain outside today. He told me the other day, that me you and Pedro were the only family he had. I just feel that a part of me is missing. I love him like a brother.

Then Nick said you'll be alright brother. We'll report it to the guard's this evening if we don't hear from him. Give him a chance to get far away from here first. Let's make up his bed, so the guards don't ask any questions, okay said Nick.

Lopez was making Romans bed, when a knock came at the door, when he turned around and looked. It was Chi co and his friends, Chi co said Nick you guys won't be able to play baseball today, because it is raining outside today. So Nick does you and your brothers want to play some pool.

I'll make you a deal, the best out of ten games. If you win six out of ten, I will take the trash out all next week, but if you lose you know the deal, then Nick said you're going down Chi co. Chi co said, it's good to have you back Nick. I'm glad things are back to normal.

Let's go, Lopez looked at Pedro and said what Chi co meant by saying that. I don't know said Pedro. Then Pedro said how you play pool Lopez. I know we can swim in a pool, but how do you play with it. Never mind said Lopez, please not now Pedro. I have a lot on my mind right now; let's just go watch them play.

As Lopez and Pedro were walking down the hallway, Pedro kept repeating to himself, shut up Pedro, shut up. When Lopez and Pedro entered the arcade room, Nick told them to sit down and be quiet. When Nick and Chi co got done playing, Chi co said to Nick you beat me seven out of ten games. Let me make you another deal.

Nick after lunch, let's get everyone down to the gym and they can watch me and you play one on one and who ever loses four out of seven basketball games will have to take the trash out for a whole month, you got a deal said Nick.

As everyone went to lunch, Lopez said to Pedro something is going on, because Nick is sitting with Chi co and his friends. It doesn't bother him that Roman is gone. Listen to me; I'm going to leave lunch early. I have a bad feeling about Roman, so I am going to the chapel and pray for Roman. So tell Nick I will be down after I get done.

Pedro replied I miss Roman to Lopez, ask god to bring him back to us. I will Pedro said Lopez. When Lopez left, Pedro decided to go and sit with Nick and his friends. When Pedro seen that there was no room to sit with Nick, he sat at the far end of the table.

Nick didn't realize that Pedro was able to hear their conversation. He heard Nick say I'm glad that loser is gone. I'm glad you told me Chi co, because I would had killed him myself, if he didn't leave last night. Then one of Chi co friends whispered to Nick, your brother is at the end of the table, as Nick turned his head to look at Pedro.

Nick noticed Pedro was looking right at him. Nick got nervous. Then everybody got quiet. Pedro got up from his chair and walked up to Nick and said Roman is no loser, but every one of you are.

Nick I only have one thing to say to you. Mrs. Connors was right about you. You are a monster. Then Nick quickly got from his chair and took Pedro to the other side of the lunch room and said Pedro please don't tell Lopez what I said about Roman, give me until the night and I will go and find Roman and bring him back.

Please promise me you won't say nothing to Lopez, you got until the night, Nick said Pedro or Lopez will hate you forever. Then Chi co yelled across the lunch room and said, are you ready Nick. Then Nick said to Pedro lets go down to the gym together and you can watch me beat this clown okay. Pedro said, let's go.

What would happen next would be a memory that no one at the center would never forget. As everyone entered the gym, Chi co said will one of you guys go and turn the lights on, and then Nick said I will go and turn the lights on. When Nick got done, as he went back down he noticed everybody was being quiet. He said what are wrong guys, and then Pedro said you won't have to go very far to find Roman.

Roman is hanging from the basketball rim at the other end of the court. Then Pedro said I am going to go and get Lopez and go to the office and get a guard. I will be back as soon as I can, okay Nick. No one would answer Pedro, because everybody was in shock, Standing there looking up at Roman hanging from the rim.

As Pedro quickly Ran up stairs to the office he told the guard's what had happened. The guard said to the dispatch sends an ambulance to the center. Then Pedro rushes out of the office to find Lopez. When he turns the corner Lopez was coming back from the chapel. Pedro ran up to Lopez, not knowing what to say. Then Pedro said to Lopez we found Roman, come with me. Oh thank you god. Then he said to Pedro I was praying that he would come back, and then Lopez noticed that Pedro wasn't talking.

All of a sudden Lopez stopped Pedro from walking so fast, and said what wrong Pedro. You heard me Pedro, then he grabbed Pedro and turned him around he noticed that Pedro was crying.

Then Lopez heard the sirens in the front of the center, Pedro replied just follow me to the gym, please Lopez.

When Pedro and Lopez entered the gym, Lopez said why is everybody at the other end of the court Pedro and who that hanging from the basketball rim. Come with me Lopez, and I will show you Roman. As Lopez got closer, he realized that it was Roman hanging with his own bed sheet that he made into a rope.

Frozen in his own footsteps he looked up at Roman and said why would you do this to me. As Lopez watched the paramedics rush in, and brought with them a step ladder and a stretcher. One of the paramedics climbed up on the ladder to untie the sheet, as they brought Roman's body down.

Nick noticed that something fell out of Romans right hand and hit the floor and bounced behind the back of the pole. After they brought Roman down and laid him on the stretcher, then Lopez came to his senses, and walked over to the stretcher and looked down at Roman.

Lopez touched his hands and said, why are your hands so cold Roman. Then Lopez looked at one of the paramedics, and asked sir please gets a blanket for Roman, because he is cold. Then the paramedic looked at him and replied, son your friend is deceased. No said Lopez, all you have to do is give him CPR, and he will be alright replied Lopez.

I am sorry son it is too late for that said the paramedic, as they took Roman away. Lopez grabbed the stretcher and wouldn't let go. Lopez started screaming and crying, saying Roman don't leave me please. It took Nick and Chi co and one of the guards to pull Lopez away from the stretcher.

Then Nick hugged Lopez and said, please get a hold of you. I don't want to lose you to Nick said Lopez. Why did this have to happen, listen to me Lopez, Roman left you a letter, I watched it fall out of his hand as they brought him down. When no one was looking I went behind the pole and got it for you. Wait until the guards leave and you can read it OK.

CHAPTER 16

THEN THE GUARDS WALKED up to Nick and said, everyone here will have to put in writing what has happened here today, so I can put it with the information I give to our officer. So make sure everyone here does their report. When they return to their rooms, have it done before six o'clock today.

Then the guards left and went upstairs. Then Nick said, Lopez do you want to read this letter to everyone. While everybody is here, no Nick I will read it when I get back to my room. Please listen Lopez said Nick on the front of the letter it says Lopez read this to everyone.

Here is your chance Lopez, do it for Roman. Then Lopez said I'll try to read it Nick. As Lopez opened the letter, he pulled a picture out that Roman had drawn and painted. It was a picture of three angels and below the picture it said "My Three Spanish Angels" above each of the angel's heads were the names of the angels, "Nick" "Lopez" "Pedro"

Then he started reading the letter, it said Lopez my friend, by the time you find this letter, I will be in heaven with my brother Antonio. Please don't be upset with me, because do you remember our first day on the way here. I told you that you would know when this day would come.

My life would have ended a lot sooner, if I had never met you. From the first time I met you, you filled my life with hope. When we prayed that night, that was the best sleep I had for months. As Lopez was reading the letter, everyone was listening.

It was so quiet you could have heard a pin drop. Nick whispered to Chi co and said, oh what have I done. Then Chi co replied, no Nick what have we all done. Lopez was reading on, it got harder and harder for him to read, specially the part when Roman wrote and said. I felt that you took me under your wings and carried me through the darkest time of my life, and I want to thank Pedro for bringing laughter when I was down. Lopez I hope your mother likes the picture I made her because;

you guys were special angels to me. Before I go Lopez, please do me a favor, when you leave that place when you get out. Please go into town, and look up Mr. Johnson and tell him the truth. Tell Nick I wouldn't have hurt the only family I love, because if everybody was like you and Pedro we wouldn't have to go to heaven to be with angels. Thank- you for keeping my promise, Love Roman.

When Lopez got done reading the letter, he was still upset and crying, everyone remained quiet and still. Then Lopez looked around at everyone and said. I know most of you didn't like Roman, but how many of you would do what he did. There are many of you thought Roman murdered his brother, but I ask each and every one of you.

If he murdered his brother then why would he take his own life to be with his brother? Roman told me everything that really happened. I was the only one he trusted. He had no one to turn to but me. I blame myself for his death, so everybody can go back to their normal lives now. You can stop your whispering, how you guys would call him scar face. I wasn't ashamed of Roman, he was my best friend, and I'll miss him.

Then Lopez said to Pedro, let's go back to our room. As they walked by everyone, everyone bowed their heads as Lopez and Pedro walked by. As Lopez and Pedro entered their room they noticed the guards were removing Roman possessions from his closet, and stripping the bed that Roman slept on.

Lopez was still crying and talking to Pedro; Then Nick walked in the room and sat on his bed. Lopez said to him, why Roman would do this. He and I were talking about telling the police the truth about what happened to his brother, and how his step father was treating him and his brother. It's my fault he died, I should have told the law myself.

Then Nick said to Lopez, was that your promise. Not to tell anyone the truth about what really happened, yes replied Lopez. Now he's dead because of me, it's my fault he died, and I can't live with myself. Then Pedro looked at Nick and said, tell him Nick, tell Lopez whose fault it really is.

What you mean Pedro, replied Lopez. Then Pedro screamed at Nick, and then Nick said okay. I will tell him. As Nick was sitting there and telling Lopez what he had said to Roman the night before he died, when he got finished telling Lopez the truth about everything.

I'm very sorry Lopez, and then Lopez became very outraged. Lopez stood up from his bed and ran toward Nick and started beating him. Nick just sat there and couldn't get up. Then finally Pedro pulled Lopez off. Pedro said stop it Lopez, because he isn't worth it.

Your right Pedro, replied Lopez. He is not worth it. I can't believe you Nick, why would you do this to Roman, your heart has turned to stone. I can't believe I have wasted my time coming here and trying to talk to you about coming home, you are hopeless.

Mama writes you every day and you don't even open her letters, you don't even write her back.

You want to know something else, I am not afraid to say it, but if you want to choke me like you did Roman go ahead and do it.

Roman was right that day, when he said it wasn't our mama's fault. But do you really want to know the truth, since you talked Roman into killing himself. Do you want to know my opinion Nick? It wasn't only mama's fault or Mr. Clark, you're not only a thief, but you're also a murderer. I don't only want you in my life; I don't even want you in our room.

As Lopez was shouting get out Nick, a guard walked into the room and asked what is going on in here. Then Nick replied there is no problem here. I will just clear out my things out of the closet and move back to my old room. Then the guard left, and Nick was getting his things to move back to his room. Lopez was sitting with Pedro on the side of his bed still crying. When Nick got done, he got ready to leave the room, he said to Lopez and Pedro I am sorry for what has happened. Pedro you are right I have become a monster. But do my brothers still love me, we will always love you Nick, replied Lopez, but I can never accept what you have done please just go.

After Nick left, Pedro said to Lopez did we do the right thing Lopez. I don't know replied Lopez, but Nick has changed and it will take a miracle for him to change his ways. Times like this Pedro, I wish I was home with mama. I miss her so much I don't feel good Pedro.

I feel so tired I need to lie down. As the night passed, Lopez didn't realize that he was coming down with an illness from stress. When he felt that he could have helped Roman. He loved Roman so much that it was hard for him to accept his death.

The following morning, Pedro got up for breakfast; he noticed that Lopez wasn't up, so he walked over to Lopez bed. He seemed that Lopez was still sleeping. Then he said Lopez are you going to get up for breakfast. Lopez rolled over and said not today Pedro. Please Pedro, when you see me sleeping don't wake me up. Please let me sleep then Pedro replied okay.

After that Pedro left, and went down to eat. When Pedro got his tray and sat down to eat by himself. Then Nick happened to look over at Pedro, Nick noticed that Pedro was eating by himself. Nick got up and walked over to where Pedro was eating and sat down by Pedro, and asked him where was Lopez. He's up in his room sick and he is sleeping, said Pedro.

Why do you even bother to ask Nick, don't you feel that you have done enough damage. Just leave me and Lopez alone, and leave now before I call a guard over here then Nick replied okay have it your way little brother, and then Nick left. Then Nick noticed throughout the day, that Lopez wasn't showing up for lunch or supper. He also didn't go to the workshop; he didn't even go out to play.

The next day was the same way, he didn't see Lopez. The third day he didn't see Lopez until late that evening. Nick snuck up to Lopez's room while Pedro was at the workshop. As he walked up to Lopez bed he noticed Lopez was lying on his side, he whispered Lopez's name several times.

Lopez didn't respond, then Lopez rolled on his back, it frightens Nick as he noticed Lopez eyes were rolling in the back of his head. Then he quickly ran out of the room screaming all the way to the medical station. When he opened the door, he asked the nurse where the doctor was, there is something wrong with my brother Lopez.

Then the nurse went and got the doctor. The doctor and Nick quickly ran back to Lopez room. As the doctor was examining Lopez Nick kept asking the doctor what is wrong with him. The doctor replied I don't know until I get him on a stretcher and take him to the medical center.

As they took Lopez back to the medical center, the doctor told Nick that he would have to wait in the lobby, and he will be back to tell him the results. Nick waited a long time, then Pedro rushes in the door and said what's wrong with Lopez. Nick looked at Pedro and replied I don't know yet because the doctor hasn't came back out.

Then Nick said why didn't you tell me that Lopez was sick. I didn't know, because he told me not to wake him up Nick. Then Nick and Pedro was talking, then the doctor finally came out and looked at Nick and said, please sit down I need to talk to you about your brother, he has a serious illness he has suffered a shock.

He also has a case of malnutrition and dehydration. We had to put an IV in him. Then Nick said, what does those words mean doctor. after The doctor got done explaining everything to Nick. The doctor replied if Lopez doesn't eat or drink on his own soon he could slip into a coma or he could even die. Then Nick said can we please go in and see him doctor. The doctor told Nick you must understand, he can't hear you or speak to you he is in a deep state of mind.

When Nick and Pedro went in to see Lopez, they both noticed Lopez was starring out in space. Then Nick said Lopez what can I say to bring you back to me. Then Pedro said it wasn't enough what you did to Roman, but even worst to your own brother Nick.

Then Nick got very upset from what Pedro said to him. Then he rushed out of the medical center. What Nick didn't know, there was some more bad news waiting on him as he entered his room. He seen a letter lying on his bed, but there was something different about this letter. This letter had writing on the back.

It said mama's last letter, then Nick opened the letter and started reading it. It said Nick my son, I hope you will read this letter because the doctor said I am not doing so well. I feel that the lord is calling me home. Son, I can't blame you for hating me. If I could trade places with you it would be my dying prayer. But I have made some arrangements for you to get the house. Please never sell it, because this way Lopez and Pedro will always have a home to come to son.

The Connors said that if your brothers ever need a home, they would be glad to take them. Nick was reading the letter he got more and more upset. Then he rush back out of his room and down the hallway, on his way to the chapel, he noticed the doors were lock. He started shaking the door handles and the guard walked by and said, what are you doing Nick.

Then Nick replied, please open these doors, I want to go in and pray please. Then the guard said I'll be glad to open them for you Nick. Because I have never seen you want to go church. Then the guard said I'll have to wait on the outside and guard the doors, to make sure no one comes in, but make it quick. I don't want to get in trouble okay Nick.

Then Nick replied, thank- you so much, but at least give me half of an hour to pray. Then the guard said no longer okay Nick, or I'll come in and get you out. Then Nick replied okay. Then the guard opens the door and let him in.

CHAPTER 17

WHEN NICK WENT TO the altar, he kneeled down on his knees and put his hands together. Then Nick looked at the huge windows in the top of the church, and there was a cross standing in the middle of the huge window. He noticed that there were some dark clouds in the sky.

Then he started praying saying, Lord I feel so lost and defeated will you step down from heaven and talk to me, or show me a sign. I lost my papa years ago, now I am losing my mother and my brother. Roman was right, it's not mama's fault that I'm here in this place, its mine.

Then Nick started crying very hard, and then he said I don't understand what has come over me in the last few months. If I don't make it to heaven, at least let me make it back home one more time to tell mama I'm very sorry.

If there is ever a time, let me be punish, not Lopez. I am not only a thief or a murderer, I am also a liar and if Roman is in heaven tell him I am very sorry. Lord bless there will be a day that will come a time that me and my brothers and mama will be a family again.

Because for once in my life I realize that the things of this world doesn't matter, because when we have you, we have everything. Lord before I go back to church, I want to make some changes and all that I am asking you is that you will protect us when the time comes. Then Nick laid his head on the altar crying, and a few seconds later he felt something warm touching his back.

Then Nick slowly lifted his head up, he noticed there was a crack in the middle of the clouds and a bright beam of sun light was shining down on him. Then a voice whisper in Nick right ear, and it said behold, I make all things new. Nick got up and walked out of the chapel. Then the guard looked at Nick and said you look like you have seen a ghost. The clouds talked to me replied Nick, please help me back to my room. I feel so tired; Nick went back to his room and lay down.

Nick felt a comfort that he never felt before. God touched him, because he knew that Nick was sincere in his heart. Nick went to sleep late that evening, then later that night. Lopez was laying in his bed then an angel looked over and seen Lopez tray on the table that the nurse left earlier that even for Lopez. To eat if by any chance that he would have woken.

The angel pushed the table and tray up to Lopez chess, and then the angel slowly put his arm under Lopez's head and lifted his head up. Then he said awake, Lopez, god has great plans for you. You eat now, and then the angel reached over and got a spoon and started feeding Lopez. When Lopez got finish eating the angel gave him some water.

During this time Lopez was trying to look at the angel's face, but the angel had a hooded cloak over his head. I haven't much time said the angel, for he has sent me to give you a message, then I must go. He said forgive your brother as he has forgiven us.

Lopez didn't realize that he was being entertained by an angel, because he replied, stranger why you are so kind to me. I also want to thank- you. If you don't mind me asking you, who are you. Then the angel put something into Lopez's right hand for him. Then the angel replied, no thank -you Lopez.

See in my time of hunger you fed me, when I was cold you gave me warmth, and in my time of darkness you comfort me. Lopez was still confused, but then as the angel step back he took his cloak down off his head. As he started fading away, he said we shall meet again someday my Spanish angel.

Lopez started screaming and said, Roman please come back. Then the nurse rushed in and said what's wrong with you. Then Lopez said please go and get Nick for me, then the nurse sent a guard down to get Nick. Then he went to Nick's room, as the guard was waking Nick up.

Nick said why you are waking me up so early in the morning. Your brother wants' to see you, said the guard. Nick said what does Pedro wants this time of the morning. Not Pedro! Said the guard, it's your brother Lopez that wants to see you.

Nick didn't hesitate; he jumped up and ran out of the room without putting his socks on or his shoes. He ran in the medical center and seen Lopez sitting up in the bed. Then Nick stop and asked Lopez are you still mad at me, no replied Lopez.

Then Nick said, I thought I have lost you forever my brother, and Nick started crying. Lopez replied, come here Nick, then they hugged one another. Then Lopez whispered in Nick's ear, I have seen Roman tonight and he made it to heaven.

Then Nick said it was just a dream Lopez. Then Lopez opens his right hand. He held a picture of Roman and his brother that Roman showed him earlier in jail. Oh my god said Nick, miracles do happen. How do you know it was Roman? He doesn't have the scar on his face anymore said Lopez.

He even told me to forgive you Nick, now I am asking you can we be a family again. Yes replied Nick, I went to the altar last night Lopez. I am sorry for treating mama bad and how I did Roman. Now he answered one of my prayers by bring you back to me. I hope he will answer two more prayers for me before it's too late.

What do you mean Nick, before its two late replied Lopez. Then Nick said, while you were ill yesterday, I left here and went back to my room and I found a letter on my bed. Lopez I don't know if this is a bad time to tell you or not, but you must know. Nick started crying, tell me Nick what are you talking about, said Lopez. Okay said Nick, mama is dying, and we've got to get out of here before it is too late.

All I have to do is contact Mr. Connors and he will get us a lawyer and get us out of here said Lopez. You don't understand Lopez; said Nick by the time he gets a lawyer and gets us out, it will be too late. If mama dies, I have no reason to live for, neither do you Lopez I want to go back to church, but first I want to clean the evil out of there before I go back.

I have a plan Lopez, are you with me. Do you have enough faith in god when the time comes? Do you believe he will protect us for what I am about to ask you to do.

Tell me Nick, said Lopez. Then Nick replied in the back of the building is a storage unit where they keep the sporting goods at, and they have some bicycles to, that they use for hiking in the summer time. All we have to do is disassemble them and sneak them under the fence.

Then we will hide them in the weeds and put them back together when the time comes. How will we get pass the guards said Lopez. What about at night time when the guards check and see if we are in bed at night. Listen to me Lopez, I have an answer to every problem don't worry okay.

I've got everything covered, all I have to do is get Chi co and some of his guy's to sneak down stairs, and get two or three mannequins out of the work shop and have them put in our bed's at nights", like I said Lopez let me handle the problem's okay, but there is one more favor," what all does Mr. Connors has and sells in his store.

While Lopez was sitting there telling Nick what he needed to know, then Nick said, Lopez I need to whisper something in your ear. And when Nick got done whispering in Lopez ear, then Lopez jerked back and said, are you crazy Nick, keep it down Lopez, Please just listen to me,".

I can't break into his store he's like an angel to us, and he'll never forgive me," said Lopez. If he is a real man of god, he will forgive you, and he will understand," this has to be done Lopez, it's been going on to long this way, we will find out," who fears god and who doesn't fear god, and who believes and who doesn't believe, and who has faith, and," then Lopez interrupted and said, okay Nick okay. I get your point,

But you better promise me no harm shall come to Mr. and Mrs. Connors or the pastor and his wife, you hear me Nick. Where is your faith at Lopez, said Nick, and you been telling me that mama said to you that god says to her, there's a reason for all thing's, god has brought Roman back to you, and you back to me, and before this is over with,.

I feel that god will bring us back together as a family, after all Lopez," they have made our church a den of thieves, and we are going there just to clean it up, now I ask you to keep your faith in god and your trust in me. Then Nick looked out the medical center window and said to Lopez.

Day light has broken, and I have a lot to do today, give me your size of your shirt and your pants and we have to get Pedro's sizes to, I've already have mine made, the suits that we will be wearing. Will be white as snow and trimmed in gold, and the blazers will be long,"

And I'll have them ready by tomorrow night, and when Nick looked back over at Lopez, and he seen he fell back asleep, then Nick got up and pulled the cover up on Lopez, and then he bent down and kissed Lopez on the forehead and said thank-you Jesus for giving me my brother back to me.

Then he went back to his room and lay down and slept until breakfast. Later that morning Chi co woke Nick up and said," Nick we don't want you to miss having breakfast with us, thanks Chi co for waking me up, because me and you and the guy's have to have a talk,.

I heard the great news this morning, the guard told us that Lopez was feeling better, said Chi co, yes but I have some more bad news, I will tell you about it on the way down to breakfast," said Nick. While Nick and the guys where whispering about the plans that Nick had," and eating breakfast,

Pedro walked in and got his tray and walked up to where Nick was at, and said," I am going back up to have breakfast with Lopez," because they took him back to our room, and he wants' to see you after you get done having breakfast," then as Pedro walked away, he turned around and said, it's good to have you back Nick, and then Pedro smiled and walked away.

Then Nick said I have everything figured out, but one thing. I guess mine and Lopez and Pedro old shoes will have to do, to wear with our new outfits, well what kind of shoe's do you got to have," said Chi co, then Nick said, three brand new pairs of white slipper's.

Then everybody got quiet, then Chi co said, well Nick, why don't you go on up and see your brother's," if you are done eating, because we got to get busy," I'll do that said Nick. After Nick left, Chi co has a plan of his own, he told everybody to pitch in some money to get Nick and his brother's some new shoes,

And they were going to give Nick, Lopez, Pedro, a surprise party the next night before they plan to runaway. All that day, Nick and Chi co stayed busy working and sewing the suits together, while some were keeping the guards occupied down in the gym playing basketball with them.

Four of the boy's went out back of the center and got two of the bicycles out of the storage units and took them apart and put them on the other side of the fence and hid them in the bushes. Three of the other boy's went down stairs and brought up three mannequins and hid two of them in Lopez and Pedro's closet and one in Nick's closet.

After everyone got done they went back to their rooms," Nick went to Lopez and Pedro's room to talk to them about their escape tomorrow night. Later on in the day Chi co and his friends came to Lopez and Pedro's room and knocked on the door may we come in they said, yes come on in said Lopez. Chi co and his friend's went in and shut the door behind them, hey Nick are you and your brother's going to play us a good game of basketball before you leave tomorrow night, said Chi co, after dinner I'll play you," said Nick let's play a quick game now chicken, said Chi co.

You're on Chi co let's, go; you're going down, then Nick laugh. As Nick and his brother's and Chi co and his friends got to the basketball gym, Nick said how are you going to play without the lights on.

CHAPTER 18

T HEN CHI CO SCREAMED out," hit the lights and when the lights came on, everybody screamed out, Merry Christmas and a happy New Year.

Nick and his brother's were shocked to see four tables set up with four large cakes and plenty of ice cream and soda pop and about fifty boxes of pizza's, then Chi co said guy's show Nick and his brother's what we got them for their Christmas gift, Chi co said we're sorry we used news paper,.

Because we didn't have any Christmas wrapping paper, and here's three smaller gifts for you guys to, Chi co wasn't paying attention, until he looked at Nick, why are you so quiet, then Nick said, because I feel that I'm leaving my family behind, and going to be with my family.

It doesn't make any sense, because I love each and every one of you and I'm going to miss you guy's very much," and another thing is that me and my brother's have never been invited to a Christmas party or any party or received any gifts before, but can I ask you guy's one question,

How did you guy's pull this off, if you guys don't mind me asking? Then Chi co said we asked the guards since it was close to Christmas if we could go ahead and have a party," they said as long as we clean our mess up, they didn't mind, so everybody here agreed to pitch in.

And we ordered all this, it was delivered here, all but the gifts we got you and your brother's we paid the one of the guards to drive down town and get your gifts, but we mostly did it for Lopez, to show our apology for what we did to Roman, and Lopez we are so sorry for how we treated him.

We had a special cake made for you, and we wanted to give you the honor of cutting it, but we all are eating the pizza's," first Pedro screamed out, as everybody said the lord's prayer, they started eating, as everyone was eating, Lopez walked over to look at Roman's cake," he looked down at it, and it said Roman Gabriel and under it, it said our guardian angel, and it had a picture of an angel looking down from the clouds.

Then Lopez walked over to where Nick and Chi co was eating pizza Lopez said to Chi co when I first came here, I didn't like you, but where are you going to live, when your time is up here, back in the streets where I was before I came here why, said Chi co, since Roman went to heaven.

Will you please come and live with our family," said Lopez, do you really mean it Lopez, said Chi co," I know I do," said Nick. For once in my life I have a new home to go to and a new family to live with, said Chi co.

Then everybody ate pizza and when they got done, they had cake and ice cream and soda pop, and when everybody got done," Chi co said, it is time for my new brother's to open their gifts. The brother's quickly opened their gifts, wow said Nick, my first new pair of white dress slipper's and they fit me how did you guys know what size I wore. I sent one of the guys up to your room when you guys weren't in there, said Chi co.

And they looked in the closet and they got the size off of your old shoes," said Chi co. Hey Lopez I got a new white belt to match my new white shoe's said Pedro, me too said Lopez. When everybody got done with the Christmas party, they cleaned their mess up, and Nick said I wanted to thank-you guys once again.

For as long as I live I shall never forget this night, you guys have more understanding and love in your hearts, than most of the people that goes to the church that me and my family goes, to all of you are angels in my book. then a guard came down and said, boy's," party time is over," it's time to hit the hay stack, good night for now.

As Nick and Chi co walked up the step's together, listen to me Nick, said Chi co, we have everything ready for you, tomorrow night, we have two bicycles on the other side of the fence," we only got two because you said Pedro don't know how to ride a bike, and there's a wrench inside a tote bag for you to put them back together.

And also a flashlight and some heavy sweaters in case you guys get cold, and some snacks and some sun glass in case you have to go put them on in the daylight, and you and your brothers new suits are wrapped in plastic bags for you to take with you. I don't know what you have planned, but may god be with you guys, oh he will said Nick,

Everybody went to sleep that night, the following morning after breakfast, the warden got on the intercom and said, when everybody is done having breakfast we have a Christmas special in the auditorium. For every one of you today, we are going to have classics like, white Christmas, the scrooge, and the Grinch.

And many more and since you all been a good bunch of guys this year, we are going to let you young men watch these classics until nine o'clock tonight and remember to enjoy this Christmas weekend and after every movie we will have cookies and refreshments for everyone.

And also remember to attend church in the morning at ten o'clock, and may god bless you, and remember Merry Christmas and have a Happy New Year, Nick whispered to Chi co and said, this is great, while everybody is watching the movies this evening, and plus the guards will be watching the them too," me and my brothers can sneak out of here about seven o'clock.

So Chi co you know the drill with the mannequins," okay I am ready anytime you are Nick," said Chi co. So while everybody was watching the movies, Nick got up out of his seat and said to one of the guards, can me and Chi co go outside since the weather is nice and pitch some balls.

The guard said, go ahead, instead Nick and Chi co went and got the boys new suits and new shoes and went outside, and under the fence into the bushes, and put the bicycles together, and they put the clothes and the shoes in the tote bag and after they got done they went back inside and watch the movies.

As it got later and later, some of the boys got bored with the movies, so some asked if they could go and play basketball and some went to the pool hall, some even went to their rooms to take a nap, Chi co said to Nick. I got to go to the restroom," and after that I'll see what time it is, and when Chi co got back he told Nick the time is five minutes till seven.

Then Nick whispered to Lopez and Pedro, my brothers it is time to go, not yet said Pedro, I want to finish watching Rudolph the red nose reindeer, this is your third time watching it today," said Nick," I like watching the island of misfits because it reminds me of you and Lopez, said Pedro.

Why not you said Nick," then Pedro said, I'm perfect, then Chi co and Nick and his brothers got up and left the auditorium, and went to the back door of the center, as they were standing at the back ready to leave, Nick looked at Chi co and said," I guess this is it, my friend," do you have to leave now," said Chi co, yes said Nick.

My mother is dyeing; please understand me, if I don't leave now. I feel that I will never get to see her alive again Chi co,

Drop me a few lines every now and then okay," said Chi co, I will said nick, then the brothers left and said good-bye to him, and once they got on the other side of the fence, Nick said to Lopez," listen to me, it takes only about an hour to drive here.

I figure it will take us about two and a half to three hours to get back home, if we don't stop, so I will double Pedro on my bicycle, so keep up with me, okay lets go, the brothers rode the bicycles for a long time, then Pedro said to Nick, this is a lot of fun, shut up Pedro and enjoy the ride," said Nick, then about an half an hour later Pedro said, my butt is starting to hurt.

Can we stop for awhile, no said Nick, we're just a half mile from the home because there's the

Dairy Queen okay, just hurry up said Pedro, they got to the mouth of the street, were they live on Nick said to Lopez and Pedro, listen to me, we will go the back way and sneak in the back yard, so be very quiet, don't make a sound so the neighbors can't hear us.

As the boys went in the back yard, and they snuck in the basement window, Nick said, whatever you guys do, don't turn any of the lights on, then they went up stairs into the living room, then Nick said, pull down the blinds and close the curtains, listen guys, said Nick,.

We will wait until early morning to take a shower, and then Nick whispered to Lopez and said where does mama keeps the back door key to the Connors store. I'll get it said Lopez," then Nick looked at Pedro and said Pedro, me and Lopez has to make one more run, and we will be back soon.

I don't care what you guys do, I'm going to lie on this couch, because my butt is sore, then Nick and Lopez left about an hour and a half later, they came back with three shot guns, and they noticed Pedro was sleeping, and then they went back out and brought the bicycles in.

I am tired said Lopez, we didn't do too bad," said Nick, all together it took two and a half hours to get here from the center and a hour and a half to take care of business, four hours all together, and it's only eleven o'clock, I'm going to set the alarm clock for seven o'clock in the morning.

Lets go to sleep for now, don't forget to say your prayers Lopez, good-night the alarm went off at seven o'clock the next morning, then Pedro looked over and said," what are those guns doing here," Nick said to Pedro, we got to have a little talk Pedro, after Nick got done explaining to Pedro," Pedro said to him," are you crazy Nick," we could be put in prison for the rest of our lives for doing something like this.

We are already prisoner's of life said Nick, people has always looked down on us in this life, please try to understand me my brother's, I can't live, if mama dies, I just want to prove to her I was sincere about serving god, and if something goes wrong. I just want us to be ready to meet her in heaven.

But why the guns," said Pedro, then Nick said, it's like this my little brother, what would mama do when our house got messy, let me tell you, what she would do, she would get the broom and sweep it up, wouldn't she," she would use a broom Nick, not a gun, said Pedro," you are missing the whole point," said Nick, the church has been in a mess for a long time,".

We are going there this morning to clean it out," now do as I say, you will follow my steps, because we are going to make our mama proud," now get up stairs and get your shower, then after we get our shower's," let's get our new clothes and our new shoes on,

When everybody got done taking their shower's," then they put their new clothes on, Lopez said, we look like movie star's, because this is the best we ever looked, we still have less than a hour to go to church.So let make us something to eat before we go, said Nick.

I also noticed when I was in the basement this morning," there's a new washer and dryer, and over by the couch is a telephone, and it work's too, were did they come from, and all those gifts said Nick,

The day you went to court, mama thought that you were going to get to come home, mama baked you a cake, and the church had you a surprise birthday party replied Lopez. But everybody got disappointed when you didn't come home.

Then Lopez said," Mr. and Miss Conner's goes to our church, they felt that mama needed help, so they bought mama a new washer and dryer, and they also got her a phone, so that mama could call you Nick, and they also sent a maid over to help mama keep the house clean,.

Mr. and Miss Conner's are good people there is a lot of good people that goes to our church Nick," so are you sure you want to do this.

After this day," said Nick, we will find out who is good, and who is bad, we will separate the lamb's from the wolves, today I promise you guys, since were done eating," said Nick, once we step out of the front door, for there will be no turning back, I will carry Pedro's gun with mine until we reach the front of the church.

Remember Lopez, keep your gun hid under your blazer, whatever you do don't drop it, because it may go off, Pedro you will walk on my right side and Lopez on my left, once we are in the church, you guys keep your mouth shut, I will be the one who does the talking," so do you guys understand me,".

Lopez and Pedro said yes Nick," we understand you, I have two warnings for you guys, I have come too far for this, my first warning you two better not mess up, or I will shoot you both myself," and my second warning, don't even think about backing out you guys know the answer to that one do we have an understanding. Then Lopez and Pedro got scared and said yes again," we understand. Then Nick said today we will make history in this town, we will give them a memory that will never be forgotten, just think today is Sunday Dec, 23, a day before Christmas eve, so here's the sunglasses that Chi co gave me, before we left the center," get them on so no one will recognizes us, it is five min, till ten,.

So by the time we get there, everybody will be seated by then.

CHAPTER 19

THE BROTHERS LEFT THE house and began walking down the sidewalk on the way to the church, and on the way there none of the brothers spoke to one another, until they walked into the parking lot of the church, everybody's here today including Mr. Clark," said Nick,.

Then as the brothers walked up to the door's Nick said to Pedro, put the guns under your blazer, then Lopez said," they are singing Christmas songs do you hear how loud they are. On my count, one, two, three, let's go in," said Nick. Then Nick opened the doors and Lopez and Pedro quickly walked in, and Nick locked the door behind them.

As Nick and his two brothers stood there, no one even noticed they came in, because everybody was singing so loud, but everybody did notice for some strange reason the pastor stopped singing," they also noticed that he was steering at the front doors," then everybody slowly quit singing.

And they turned their heads around to see what the pastor was steering at. Every one notice the strangers were just standing there in their white suits, with their black sunglasses on, and all three of them holding their hands inside their blazers.

Then the pastor said," would you gentlemen like to take a seat and enjoy our service. Then Nick hesitated and said no thank-you," but we are here to take care of some business," what might that be. Replied the pastor do any of you remember us, said Nick, then they took their glasses off, and some of the school kids started laughing and whispering," ooh we better watch out, the beggar's are back.

Then Nick looked to his right, then to the left," then all three brothers pulled out their shot guns from under their blazers at the same time, then everybody got quiet again," and one of the church members said, oh my god they are here to kill us.

Then Nick said, I only have three messages for all of you, this is to those who doesn't fear god, but fears me, and to those who fears me, doesn't fear god, then Nick drew back his gun and cocked it, and then he said, this is to those who fear death.

Then all of the sudden people started to panic, and some were dramatized, there were three windows on each side of the church, and there was also a door in the back of the church, one third of the members raised the windows up and climbed out and some jumped out, and one third of the members rushed out of the back door.

Including Mr. Clark and his wife Mrs. Clark took his hat and covered his face as he went out the back door, then after all the excitement settled down; the three brothers were still standing there. Bye the front doors, then they slowly started walking down the middle of the isle.

The three brothers noticed, about one third of the members remained in their seats, as they were walking, Pedro aimed his gun to the right," and Lopez aimed his gun to the left, and Nick aimed his gun forward, then Pedro heard someone whispering his name,

As Pedro looked over," he seen George sitting in the third row from the alter," then Pedro whispered very low and said," I love you papa, I'll see you in heaven, and George noticed that Pedro was sad when he said it, because he wasn't smiling, then George realized, thinking to himself, that this was Eldora's vision.

But instead of the three brothers holding the guns in Eldora's dream, they were holding sword's, and George also noticed, either though the brothers didn't have wings, George did noticed the suit's they were wearing had a special glow to them, As the three brothers were still walking towards the alter Lopez would look to his right and then to his left.

He seen some of the members down on their knee's saying their last prayer's," and fathers and mothers holding their small children, covering over them with their bodies, and some were in hysterics, then what really bothered Lopez when he heard a little girl say to her mother, mommy please don't cry, we will get to have Christmas in heaven.

As the brothers approached the podium," Nick looked up at the pastor, Nick seen that the pastor was trembling as the tears were coming down his face," because the pastor knew in his heart, that he had preached his last message.

But what happened next's," surprised everyone there," Nick said to the pastor, forgive us for bringing guns into the church, but we just wanted to clean out the hypocrites, so we can start serving god.

Then the three brothers kneeled down on the floor and laid their guns in front of the alter, and then Nick looked up at the pastor, and started crying, and said pastor will it be all right," if me and my brothers pray for our mama to get well, then the pastor looked down and said, I will come down and pray with you and your brothers.

And we all shall pray for our sister Eldora, then everyone got up out of their seats and started walking toward the alter to pray with the three brothers," except George, because he heard the sounds of sirens coming from the police car.

As they approached the church, then George realized that was the end of Eldora vision, when he looked out the windows and saw the flashing amber's light's, then George heard one of the officer's get on the bull horn and say," we have you surrounded, release the hostages,".

And lay down your weapons and come out with your hands on top of your head's we will only give you fifteen minutes to reply," we are armed. And we will come in and get you," mean while the El Paso news teamed arrived on the scene," and asked what was going on.

The next thing that happened every television station was interrupted throughout the state of Texas, because in the hospital were Eldora was at," Maria was sitting beside her bed, watching the television, then all of the sudden the program went off the air.

And the news came on," a news man said," we interrupt this program with a special news bulletin," we have just received news that three young brothers has escaped from the correctional center for boy's late yesterday evening, and this morning on the out skirts of El Paso, the three young men.

Has taken a church captive and it's member's they are being held hostage, at this time, eyewitness has told, that the kidnapper's are armed and very dangerous, the kidnapper's names are Nicholas Santos, age sixteen, Lopez Santos, age fourteen, and Pedro Santos, he is only nine years old.

When Eldora heard her sons names on the television she raised up on the bed, and jerked off the oxygen mask, and said to Maria, I have to go there now before they hurt my son's, I'm sorry Eldora, but I can't take you, because George has the car, and mine is in the shop, then the doctor walked in. And seen Eldora was upset, he said to her it's not good for you to get upset, and I do understand your concern for your son's, so to show you how much I care, then he said to Maria please help her to get dressed, then he said.

I have a special vehicle that is equipped with a wheelchair," and when you are ready, I will take you myself," oh god bless you doctor," said Eldora, but mean while, up town at the fire department.

Tom was watching the news's," then he look at his men and said, I don't believe what I'm hearing, I don't know the oldest brother, but I do know the other two and I just can't sit here and watch my little man get hurt," there has to be a reason for all of this, we have a Christmas parade today around noon.

And I never forget the joy in his little eyes when I told him, that I wanted him to ride with us, and I feel that it's my duty to go over and rescue him, I'm always been a man of my word," I made him a promise that I would protect them.

So do I have any volunteers, then all the firemen stood up, then Tom said, "I am proud of all of you men that you feel the same way I do, so let's saddle up and go, and get our little commander.

Back at the church, the brother's were still praying for their mother, and then George walked up to the pastor and said, sir I don't mean to interrupt the prayer, but ten minutes already passed, and in five more minutes. They may kick the door's down and come in and get these boy's.

Because the law believes that we are being held hostage, George I will need you and a couple of the saint's said," the pastor to stay in here and pray with the brother's, while I step out and talk to the authorities.

Then the pastor and all of the saint's," but three walked up to the door's and unlocked them, as they opened the door's for as far as the eye's could see there were thousands of people standing around to see the invent that was taking place.

Then the pastor noticed, that several people were rushing up the sidewalk, the pastor quickly got the saints out of the church, and they locked the door's behind them, the El Paso news lady and sergeant Santa z, and Tom from the fire department came up to the pastor," .

Sergeant Santa z was being very rude, because he wouldn't give the pastor or any one a chance to talk, then all of a sudden, a police officer ran up to the sergeant and said sir, the two sniper's we have up in the tree's want to know, since most of the hostage are out of the church.

They said they have a clear shot at the kidnapper's, do you want them to take them out, No! Shouted the pastor, don't you dare hurt those young men," no crime has been committed but a miracle has taken place here today, and I can guess who started all the gossip, is all the hypocrites that ran out of the church with their tails between their legs.

And these people behind me, are true saint's of god, and if those hypocrites had half the faith, those young men up at the altar has, they would be in there praying with them, instead of being liars, and those people are not welcome to our church until they can show us, the same faith that our saints, and those three young men has.

And if these young men are guilty so are we, then the pastor said, take me and then the pastor's wife said the same, take me too, and each one of the saint's repeated one after another, take me.

Then all the people, that were watching the event taking place, started getting angry and chanting, let them go! Let them go! They kept repeating it, then the sergeant said, pastor, if you and your people don't move out of our way, I will have to arrest you all for obstructions justice, so move out of the way.

And let me and my men do our job, please, and as Tom was standing there, he noticed that some of the saint's were crying, Tom couldn't handle it, so he knew that he had to do something, quickly, so Tom looked at the sergeant with a smile and said very nicely," can I barrow your bull horn for a few seconds please.

Why sure Tom, you're welcome to use it, and then Tom said," thank-you sergeant, then the sergeant was shocked," when he heard what Tom had to say, Tom got on the bull horn and said, now hear this," all the firefighter get your axes, and block the entrances of the church, and guard the saints at all cost.

The firemen did as Tom asked, and then the sergeant looked at Tom and said, what are you doing Tom? Then Tom said, I am taking charge of this case," and one more thing, I am going to my truck to get a chainsaw, and if those sniper's isn't out of those tree's by the time I get back, I will cut those tree's down with your men up there.

You wouldn't dare, said the sergeant, watch me," said Tom then Tom left, and when he got back, as he started cutting down the tree, everybody started laughing and chanting, cut it down, cut it down,.

Everybody watched the tree come down, with the sniper jumping out of the tree before it hit the ground, as Tom got ready to cut down the other tree," he sees no reason to cut it down, because the other sniper jumped down quickly, after he saw what Tom did to the first tree.

And when Tom got done, he walked back over, to the pastor and said, I am very sorry for cutting your tree down, but I will gladly pay you for it, don't worry about it sir, because it was well worth it to me, then the pastor started laughing. And Then sergeant Santa z, walked up to Tom and said," don't you realize those young men has gun's in there, and you better hope the news papers don't get a hold of this," and our men against one another, so tell me Tom what will the press have to say.

Tom got very angry and said," This has nothing to do with our men being involved, this has to do with me and you," and as far as any gun's, I haven't heard any shot fired yet. You know the truth," they are in there praying for their mother, and then Tom whispered and said,"

As far as the press goes, you won't be around, to read it tomorrow, because the press will make me out to be a hero, when I put you in the obituary if you harm any one of those young men in the church.

CHAPTER 20

YOU OR NO ONE is going to stop me, from doing my job, and why are you and your men doing here anyway, I don't see any fires, said sergeant Santa z, listen to me said Tom," I made a promise to a couple little men in there that I will protect them.

Then sergeant said, just a few minutes ago, I been informed that the mayor and the judge are on their way down here, they'll get those church doors open, and you and no one will stop me from going in there, and get those three little devils.

And beside Tom, don't you got a parade to attend, it's almost noon, then Tom walked away, as Tom and the pastor was talking, they noticed the crowd was still chanting, let them go, everything was starting to quite down, because as the men looked on they noticed that a line in the crowd was starting to form on each side.

And in the middle of the crowd, was a doctor pushing Eldora in a wheelchair, and Maria was walking along the side of them, and when they got up to the church door's, Eldora looked up at sergeant Santa z and said can, I please go inside the church.

And spend some time with my son's, before they are taken away from me again, then sergeant Santa z said, yes you may, then the pastor unlocked the doors, then the doctor continue to push Eldora in, and then Maria walked in.

And once again, the pastor locked the door's again behind them, then the doctor pushed Eldora toward the alter George and the two saint's and the three boys were sitting in their seats, as soon as Lopez and Pedro seen their mama," they got up and out of their seats and ran up to Eldora.

And started giving her kisses and hugs and telling her how much they loved her and missed her, then Nick got up and started walking towards his mama, and he kneeled down on the floor in front of her lap, and then he said that god has answered my prayers.

I have got to see you one more time before they take me away," mama I am so confused, I don't know what to say, just say you still love me son," said Eldora, then Nick said, I shall always love you mama, then the pastor came into the church and locked the door's behind him.

He whispered to George, I am sorry, but the family only has one minute to be together, because sergeant Santa z has with him," the united states marshals, and I will have to let them come in, I understand said, George.

Then George told Eldora and the boy's what was going to happen, Eldora looked at her three sons and said, Jesus please don't let them hurt my children," then she started crying and said to her son's kneel and pray with me now.

As they started praying, George noticed a bright halo around Eldora and the boy's, and then George noticed two minutes went by, and the pastor left the doors unlocked. For the law to come in, then George looked at his watch again, three minutes went by.

Eldora and the boy's stopped praying Eldora looked at George and said, what is going on, I don't know said, George, the people outside stopped chanting," them both of the church doors opened," but not with the law coming in, it was the pastor and the saint's on one side and Tom and his men the other side.

With his men rushing in, the pastor said to Eldora, God sure does work in mysterious ways, because there are two very important people wants to meet you and your son's, then Tom put Pedro on his shoulders, and every one walked outside.

Then as soon as they stepped out of the church," the people started chanting, again, let them go, George, Eldora, Maria, and the three boy's noticed, there was a big white limousine, in front of the church and they also noticed, that the U.S Marshall's were getting in their vehicles and drove away.

The mayor and the judge of el Paso walked up to Eldora and interduced themselves and they said, to Eldora, we need your help Mrs. Santos the governor of Texas has asked us, to have you to speak to the people, because we are receiving thousands of phone calls a minute. They are repeating themselves and screaming over the phone, let them go, let them go, they are driving us crazy, please help us. Because we feel that we will have a riot on our hands, and we don't want that during the holidays. If we grant your son's their freedom, will you be satisfied.

Oh yes more than anything," said Eldora, then the judge said," Miss. Santos, would you and your son's please stand in front of me just for a minute, I won't take long, as Eldora and her son's step forward in front of the judge, then the judge whispered to sergeant Santa z and said, hey you idiot, give me your bull horn now.

The judge got on the bull horn, and said, I have been given the power by the governor in the state of Texas, and the authority to declare, Nicholas, Lopez, and Pedro Santos, not guilty, then the crowd stopped chanting," and started cheering for joy.

The judge looked at Eldora and said, me and the mayor has to go to a Christmas party, because the election is around the corner, I would appreciate if you would cast your votes for us, oh I will vote for you," your honor, said Eldora.

And then the judge said, to Eldora, my church is on the other side of town, and we have been having problems there, you wouldn't mind if I borrow your son's for one Sunday would you, then the judge started laughing," then the judge and the mayor said, we wish you and your son's a Merry Christmas and a Happy New Year.

Then Tom and the pastor and George over heard the judge saying to the sergeant Santa z, I hope you enjoy your Holidays without pay, and if you decide to come back. You are welcome to traffic duty," you idiot, then George and the pastor and Tom started laughing.

Pedro walked up to his mama, and said," mama you got your Christmas wish, we will have Nick home with us for Christmas, George said, to Eldora, how do you feel Eldora, I feel well since I got my son's back with me," said Eldora.

This calls for a celebration said, George, I want you guys and your mama to go to my house, we'll have a big Christmas party," but first, I'm going Christmas shopping for all of you first, then Pedro said, I'm very sorry mama, but I can't go with you right now, Mr. Tom and the guy's need me to lead the fire trucks in the parade, I hope you understand mama.

I understand son, said Eldora, I know you are the commander," then Tom said," I will bring him to George's house as soon as the parade is over, I will take good care of him, I know you will said Eldora," then a detective by the name of Mr. Johnson walked up to Lopez and said, I been informed that you may have some information about Roman that might help me,".

The information will help you sir," said Lopez, then the detective said, would you like to wait after the holidays, no, said Lopez, if I tell you, can I go with you, to make sure you arrest him now, I want to make his holiday miserable, and then Lopez started crying.

And said," Sir you don't understand," I loved Roman like a brother, and sir if I could, I would like to shoot him, I can't allow you to do that. But if you had the right information, I know some people in prison that will take care of him for us.

I promise you that, is that a deal, said the detective, yes sir, let me go and tell my mama, what I have to do, and I will be right back, said Lopez, I will be waiting on you Lopez, said, the detective.

After Lopez got permission from his mama," he left with detective, then Nick said, to George," we can't leave yet, because I have to go back into the church and get something, please wait on me,.

And when he came back out," he was caring the three shot guns, George looked at Nick and said, be very careful with those, you might accidentally drop one, and it could go off and shoot somebody, don't worry sir," then Nick opened the chamber, of each gun.

And there were no bullets in none of the guns then he said to George, do you think I would let Pedro carry a gun with a bullet in it, I don't think so, then George laughed and said, I certainly hope not.

And then George said, if you don't mind my asking, but those guns look very familiar, that's what I need to talk to you about sir, said Nick, when Nick got done explaining himself, then Nick said, I also want to apologize for the way I talked to you.

When you first brought mama out to see me," what Nick said next," surprised George, when Nick said do you forgive me papa, then George said, don't worry about it son, then they hugged one another. As everyone was getting into their vehicles, Nick said, to his mama, let me talk to the pastor and his wife before we leave.

Then Nick walked over to the pastor and his wife, and said, I just wanted to say," I'm sorry for all the problems I have caused you and your wife today, don't be sorry," said the pastor, I am one who should be sorry," you gave me a wakeup call.

Because I knew of all the bad things that were going on in our church, and I want to thank-you for putting a stop to it, you and your brothers were like David in the bible, you young men stood up against giants, "and you all won and what happened here today, will go down in history.

And you made me proud, because you made me part of it, thank-you pastor said Nick, as Nick turned around to go back to George's car, a lady reporter rushed up to Nick and said," can we get a comment from you, about what happened today, Nick looked into the camera and said," I can only say, I want to give god the praise and glory, for watching over me and my family.

And if my other family is watching me, I want to thank-you guy's for your help, that made this possible, and I also want to say to a special friend out there, that I can't mention his name because I don't want to get him in any trouble.

But you know who I'm talking about, you know where your home is at when you get out, until then, I want to say, I wish you guy's a Merry Christmas. And Chi co and every one at the center was watching, Nick on the television set, and then he looked around the room and whispered hey that's my brother, to the television set then he said, Merry Christmas to you too Nick.

That's pretty much the end of the story," all but a few details, things went back to normal, on the outskirts of El Paso, Lopez's dream came true, that day the detective arrested Roman's stepfather, they didn't pull right in front of his house, they parked three houses down from his instead, Mr. Johnson noticed a lot of people were going in and out of Roman's old home place.

The detective called for backup, with a warrant to search the house, they didn't only get him for child abuse, but also for possession of illegal drugs," while the police were removing the drug's out of the house, detective Johnson took Roman's parents into custody.

As he placed Roman's mother in the back seat of the car, Lopez couldn't stand looking at Roman's stepfather standing there in handcuffs, and smiling at Lopez, so while the detective was busy on the other side of the car, Romans stepfather whispered to Lopez, to bad about Roman and then he started laughing.

Lopez happened to look down on the sidewalk and seen a broken tree branch, then he quickly picked it up and started beating Roman's stepfather in the face with it, and when he fell down, Lopez started stomping his chest," and he kept repeating," this is for Roman. And Antonio, then the detective grab Lopez and said, stop it Lopez you're killing him.

What are you going to do about it, said Lopez, arrest me, I've been in jail before, as the detective looked at Lopez,

He notice that he was very upset, and started crying again the detective said to Lopez, you really did care a lot about Roman didn't you.

Then he hugged Lopez, and said, let's take these guys down town and book them up, then I'll take you home okay, on the way to the police station, Roman's stepfather, said I want to press charges on that kid for hitting me.

I'm sorry sir, but I didn't see anything, I thought you fell down the steps, then he looked over and smiled at Lopez, after the detective arrested the two parents, then he took Lopez to George's house.

As the detective dropped Lopez off at George's house he said, I want to thank-you Lopez for helping me solve Roman's case," I couldn't have done it without you, and if you keep going to church and keep serving god," you may get to see Roman again someday.

Yes sir," said Lopez, I have already seen Roman again, so sir you have a happy holiday, and god bless you," and good bye, and the same to you Lopez said the detective, and then he drove away, after the holidays was over, the brother's returned to school.

And no one made fun of them anymore, they were treated with respect, as a matter of fact some of the children asked them for their autographs then a few months later. Chi co was released and he came and lived with the family.

CHAPTER 21

ON LOPEZ FIFTEENTH BIRTHDAY, George took him out, and bought him a fourteen carat gold frame for Lopez picture, that Roman made for his mama, he put it in the frame and hung it on the living room wall.

Eldora wasn't in the wheelchair very long after she got her son's back, as the years went by and when the brother's graduate, Nick and Chi co got a small job and they would save their money, because they wanted to open their own men's dress shop.

Then George came by one day to talk to Nick and Chi co, he said listen to me guys I found a building that has plenty of space, and I can help you get the sewing equipment, and I can also help you two with the bank, but the only problem is Nick you won't believe were the building is at, were is it at papa, said Nick.

It is Mr. Clark shoe store, he went out of business after the people heard how Mr. Clark treated you, so how about it, that's great papa, when can we start, said Nick," tomorrow if you want to son, said George, less than a year went by, Nick and Chi co was doing great, they were short on help.

So they hired some of the guy's from the correctional center, people came from all over to buy their clothes there, then they took down Mr. Clark's sign and put their sign up, it said, The Spanish Angel dress shop for men and woman.

The business did great, but no matter what, every one still attended church every Sunday, Nick and Chi co fell in love with two beautiful saints in the church, and both of the young men got married shortly, and later each of the wives gave birth to a baby boy.

Nick named his baby Roman Nicholas Santos, and Chi co named his baby Antonio Andros because they both had special feeling for Lopez, each day when Lopez came home from school, he would do his homework and when he got done. He would ride his bicycle over to Nick and Chi co houses.

And he would help take care of his little nephew's, as the babies got older, Lopez would take them both for a walk and sometimes to the park to play with them, and when Lopez graduates instead of wanting to be a baseball player, he decided to take up business and physiology.

Because he made up his mind when he finish college, that he was going to open a foster home for unwanted children, he wanted to do this for Roman because there wasn't a day that went by without him having Roman on his mind.

And when Pedro graduated, he would hang around the fire department so much, that Tom and the men taught him how to be a fire fighter, but his heart was filled with joy, when Tom told him one day to put up his toy fire truck, because he was going to learn how to drive a real one.

His dream came true about a month later, because Tom gave him a job, Tom also told Pedro. That one day that he would be the next fire chief commander when he retired, all the brothers started living successful lives.

And Eldora and Maria spent most of their time nursery shopping, George and Maria Connors became Eldora's grandchild's godparents, the Santos and the Connors, the pastor and his wife, and the saints would celebrate every December the twenty third of the year together.

And talked about that one special day, how god preformed his great miracles, and of all holiday's that was their most precious one.

THE END